W9-BDY-717

"Where is this new assignment going to take me?" asked John Wesley Sand. "If I accept, that is."

"Well . . . sometimes an entire planetary system can get a bad name, though in reality Hellquad isn't all that bad . . ."

"*Hellquad!*" Sand said, jumping up. "You Soldiers of Fortune halfwits want me to spacejump out to the Hellquad System, out to those four godforsaken planets on the edge of nowhere! A quartet of planets that, no matter where you start from the other three are even worse. The Hellquad System is, for good and ample reasons, known throughout the length and breadth of the rational universe as the cesspool of creation."

"Oh, they're not that bad."

"They're worse! Consider, if you will, their very names. How could anyone with even a smidgen of sense expect anything but dire trouble and bad times on a set of planets named Farpa, Fazenda, Ferridor and Fumaza?"

DAW Books
by **RON GOULART** include:

UPSIDE DOWNSIDE
BIG BANG
HAIL HIBBLER
THE ROBOT IN THE CLOSET
HELLO, LEMURIA, HELLO
THE WICKED CYBORG
CALLING DR. PATCHWORK

etc.

HELLQUAD

Ron Goulart

DAW BOOKS, INC.
DONALD A. WOLLHEIM, PUBLISHER

1633 Broadway, New York, NY 10019

Copyright ©, 1984 by Ron Goulart.
All Rights Reserved.
Cover art by Frank Kelly Freas.

Daw Book Collectors' Number 592

FIRST PRINTING, AUGUST 1984

1 2 3 4 5 6 7 8 9

PRINTED IN U.S.A.

Chapter
1

Just as the lovely four-breasted blue girl was slipping her lacy singlet up over her head, her voice changed.

It grew deep and growly, saying, "Have we got a nifty job for you, John."

John Wesley Sand sat up on the warm jellobed, knuckling his naked thigh. "Foxed again," he said, scowling up at the skyblue girl who stood close beside the quivering bed.

He was a long lanky man, thirty-three years old in Earth Standard Chronology. He's been knocked about quite a bit since we last encountered him. His sun-bleached hair is a few shades lighter, his skin more weathered and deeply tanned and there's a quirky scar snaking up his left side. This latter from a talon wound sewn up out on one of the Trinity System Planets by a brainstimmed lobsterman who suffered from palsy in both claws.

"Turn on the news," suggested Tessie Stardrake in her new deep voice.

Sand frowned. "What is it, a skullplant?"

"Can't fool you, eh, John." Tessie's amber eyes were wide and staring. She held the frilly polkadot singlet so it covered only her left row of breasts. "Yes, that's exactly how we're able to talk to you via the medium of this fetching young lady."

Sand shifted on the bed, causing it to quiver and emit low gulps. "I'm on vacation, cultivating quietude for the most part. I've been frequenting a few of the bistros here on Barnum in search of nothing more than a little gentle fun," he explained, almost patiently. "Though I'm essentially a leg man, I was intrigued when I met Tessie this evening at the Polka Paradise. Why'd you wait so long to make your damn pitch?"

"Wanted to be sure you wouldn't bolt before we spoke our piece. This way, with your trousers tossed over the barbot, your all-season skivvies dangling from yonder lightball, your—"

"You weren't controlling her earlier conversations, were you?"

"No. Tess really is quite bright and an expert on 19th Century Earth Literature."

"Damn, here I meet a young woman who's up on one of my favorite topics, she's attractive to boot, and it turns out you bastards have an SOF, Inc computer terminal planted in her skonce."

"Only a tiny one," said the deep voice through the girl's pretty blue lips. "It really does, you know, come in handy for discreetly contacting and recruiting free-lance agents for Soldiers of Fortune, Inc."

When Sand rose off the jellobed, it made a lipsmack sound and wobbled wildly for several seconds.

"I'm not planning to take on any new free-lance jobs

until way next year." He prowled the oval room for a moment, glancing out through the oneway glaz window of the chamber at the multitude of lights gleaming out there in the capital city. Then, turning, he leaped and snagged his shorts off the softly glowing globe that hovered in midroom. "For one thing, my stock in Amalgamated Skymines keeps paying me a nice dividend every—"

"Amalgamated Skymines just went kafloppo, haven't you heard?"

Sand finished pulling up his shorts before turning to stare at Tessie with narrowed eyes. "Did you guys rig something so—"

"Heavens, no!" Tessie's skyblue hand crossed both her hearts. "Honest. But seriously, John, now that you realize you aren't quite so affluent as you thought, why don't you listen to our propo—"

"How much?"

"SOF, Inc can pay you a fee of 200,000 trudollars."

"To go where?" He retrieved his trousers, got into them.

Tessie lowered her head, fingered the lace of her singlet. "Well, it's a sort of dangerous place."

"Most of the jobs I do for you occur in such locations." He scanned the room, seeking some trace of his tunic.

"Under the snaxtable," Tessie said in her deep gravelly voice.

"Ah, so you guys were watching me for quite a while before you actually made contact, huh? Playing peeping—"

"We're in here. Naturally we're going to—"

"Where is this new assignment going to take me . . . if I accept?"

"Reputation is a funny thing, John. With both planets and people. Why, sometimes a planet gets a bad name and yet there's no real reason why it should, except for rumor and falsehood," began Tessie, tracing lazy Z's on the thermorug with her blue big toe. "In fact, there are even entire planet systems that suffer from a bum reputation, though in reality they aren't all that bad. We can think, off hand, of sever—"

"No, nope, not at all," cut in Sand while yanking his tunic out from under the floating plaz table.

"But you haven't yet even heard the name of—"

"Hellquad," he said, straightening up. "You SOF halfwits want me to spacejump out to the Hellquad System, out to those four godforsaken planets on the edge of nowhere. A quartet of planets that, no matter where you start from the other three are even worse. The Hellquad System is, for good and ample reasons, known throughout the length and breadth of the rational universe as the cesspool of creation."

"Oh, they're not that bad."

"They're worse." He tugged his tunic on. "Consider, if you will, their very names. How could anyone with even a smidgen of sense expect anything but dire trouble and bad times on a set of planets named Farpa, Fazenda, Ferridor and Fumaza? Are those names to inspire either—"

"Oh, Fazenda is sort of catchy," said the voice of the SOF field recruiter. "When you say it, I see visions of rolling green fields, stately trees. Fazenda, Fazenda—"

"Grout crap," responded Sand. "I see slavers, space pirates, welfs, mewts, deadbeats, madmen, psychotic cyborgs, lunatics at large, brokedown andies, bimbos, lycanthropes, alfies, hookers, cutpurses, senile servos, zombies, the dregs of every other planet in—"

"But, John, you're only looking at the negative side."

"There's a positive side?"

Tessie told him, "Suppose we up your fee to $250,000?"

Sand reached inside his tunic to rub at his zigzagging scar. "You'll have to go to $300,000."

"Whoops!" gasped Tessie. "Now you're on the high side."

Sand located his boots in the vicinity of the jiggling bed. Settling into a rumphug chair, he pulled them on. "You've lost five men out in the Hellquad planets already. Was that all on this same job?"

"What makes you think we've lost even one Soldiers of Fortune, Inc agent out there on—"

"Even when I'm on vacation and mostly meditating, I don't turn into a nitwit," Sand said. "I hear things. I put myself in places where I can do that. Well?"

"We have, as a matter of fact, lost four of our men, yes," admitted Tessie in her gruff voice. "As to the fifth, well, we aren't quite certain. We found a little chunk of what might be him, but we have to make a few more lab tests before we come right out and notify the next of kin."

Sand grinned thinly. "If you guarantee me $300,000, I'll take the job."

"How about $250,000 plus a new dining room set and an all expenses paid trip for two to Jupiter?" inquired Tessie. "See, when it comes to perks instead of cash, we can—"

"I never work on the barter system. Cash. In front."

"Half now, half if . . . um . . . that is, when you get back here to Barnum."

"All. Now."

Tessie glanced over at the barbot, who had a digital clock in his stomach. "You're going to miss the newscast unless you stop bickering, John."

"I'm not bickering. I'm simply stating. You pay the

$300,000 before I have myself spacewarped out to the Hellquad."

"Okay, you win. You'll have the dough first thing in the morning."

"Deposit it in my account at the 1st Colony Bank." Sand pointed at the domed ceiling. "Do you still have my account number and the bank's orbit patt—"

"Yes, yes." She nodded at the vidwall, the anxious motion agitating her quartet of breasts. "Now, for goodness sake, turn on the damn 11 O'Clock Intensive News Hour. Let's just hope you haven't already missed the segment we want you to catch."

Sand, his left eye almost winking, crossed to a floating plaz viewchair. When it shaped itself to his contours, he pushed a selectbutton in the row on the chair arm.

The wall immediately in front of him came alive. There before him shimmered a six-foot-square image of two dead people in their seethru glaz coffins.

"Good, we're just in time." Tessie came up behind him.

". . . here's Ozgood Papp on the scene on the planet Esmeralda, where one of the most sensational espionage cases of our era has popped back into the limelight."

A chubby catman, clad in an Intensive News onepiece blazersuit, could be seen next to the coffins with a tokstik clutched in his paw. There were quite a few other newspeople, camerapersons and botcameras circling the pair of glaz coffins, which rested up on neowood sawhorses in the middle of a stretch of bare white flooring. Suspended over the coffins was a huge metal cone, thickly studded with tubes, tiny bulbs, dials.

". . . exactly ten ESC years ago that this infamous, or

so we thought then, couple were executed for selling defense and security secrets to a galactic federation beyond our own planet system," Papp was saying into his mike. "Yet today, because of a surprise ruling handed down by the Esmeralda Supreme Court Computer, Hazel and Jonas Brandywine are being brought back to life. The high court has ruled that they were innocent after all of espionage and have been unjustly dead for . . . will you get your blinking forepaw off my . . . That the trial of Hazel and Jonas Brandywine represents a gross miscarriage of justice. Ah, but I see the Federal Resurrector and his crew have just arrived here at the Municipal Revitalization Center. Soon now Jonas and Hazel Brandywine will be back among the living. You can be sure our IN mikes and cameras will be right up front to get their initial responses to this amazing turn of events . . ."

"Would you care to fondle me while we're watching," invited Tessie in her own voice as she lowered herself onto Sand's lap. "They say it's okay, so long as it doesn't distract you too much."

"Get off me," he suggested.

"We don't want you to feel totally deprived of any social life." The Soldiers of Fortune, Inc voice was back. "Besides, when you arrive out in the Hellquad System, the quality of feminine companionship may not be—"

"You can sit here in silence," he told the lovely blue girl. "But when I'm thinking about a $300,000 job, I don't fool around."

On the large wall screen the whiteclad resurrectionist was climbing up a ladder being held by his two lizardman associates. When he reached the cone, he scrambled into a bucket seat alongside it and started adjusting knobs, dials and switches.

". . . unfortunate note is that Jonas and Hazel Brandywine's only daughter has long since vanished from human, or any other, ken," Ozgood Papp was commenting. "Thus the gladness of Jonas and Hazel Brandywine at being brought back from the dead will be dampened some by the knowledge that in the long lonely decade since they were executed for high treason their only child has—"

"That's where you come in," said Tessie in her deep voice.

"The daughter?"

"This report was taped several hours ago on the planet Esmeralda. Since coming back to life the Brandywines have, through their attorney Sidney Harum, contacted SOF, Inc offices on their home planet and offered us a tidy sum to locate the missing girl."

"How'd your other agents get involved then?" He sat up as best he could with the blue girl perched on his lap. "If these Brandywines were dead and gone until only a few hours—"

"Their attorney suspected they'd wish to find their poor lost daughter," explained Tessie. "Once he learned of the court's decision to revive them, he contacted us. That was eleven days ago. The Brandywines themselves confirmed what Harum had told us and, we might add, raised the amount offered for the job."

"Eleven days ago, huh? Means you've been losing an agent just about every other day."

"But that'll surely change with you on the job. If we'd been able to track you down earlier, we might have saved some—"

"What's the missing daughter got to do with the Hellquad planets?"

"Since there were no next of kin, the girl was put up for adoption by the government soon after the execution of her parents," Tessie told him in the voice of SOF, Inc. "When she was thirteen, some eight years ago, she was shipped out to one of the Hellquads to live with a relative of some adoptive parents. After a while she seems to have disappeared and there's been no word of her for the past four years."

"Doubtful a girl could survive out there for eight years."

"The Brandywines want to be absolutely certain. And, because of their various Erroneous Death compensations and a substantial Resurrection Bonus, they can more than afford to hire us."

Rising and depositing the girl in the vacant chair, Sand began pacing the room. He ignored the return to life of the spy couple that was occurring on the wall.

". . . can you share with us what it feels like to be alive?"

". . . I'm Papp of Intensive News. Can you tell our millions of viewers if this is a surprise to you?"

"Did you ever imagine, as you faced the execution process, that one day . . ."

Walking back to the chair, Sand turned off the wall. He frowned down at Tessie. "Suppose the daughter is still out there. Why the devil would somebody knock off five of your agents to keep them from finding her?"

"That's one of the things we hope you'll find out."

Sand nodded. "Yeah," he agreed. "I'd better."

Chapter
2

Sand scowled as he stepped clear of the cleanbeam cabinet after his morning shower. He glanced back over his shoulder into the plaztile cubicle. "I've got a hunch . . ."

Still frowning, he walked, unclothed, out into the bedchamber of his Barnum Center Hotel suite.

From his kitbag he fetched a small silver cylinder, went back into the bathroom.

When Sand activated the cylinder and held it inside the cleanbeam cabinet, it commenced giving off a small clucking sound.

"Damn," he muttered, "who the hell planted this?"

He located the microbug up near the base of the beamnozzle. Scrutinizing the damn thing under the lenz built into the cylinder, he discovered it was a low-budget but powerful listening device of the sort manufactured in the zombie factories out in some of the boondock planets.

Sand flushed it. "Hope you enjoy the aural experience."

He then checked out the rest of his suite with the detection gadget. Attached to the underside of his quivering jellobed was a minibug. This one, of Barnum System origin, caused the bed to shimmy when he detached it.

Sand returned to the bathroom, sent the second spy device gurgling down in the wake of the first. "Have I got two different groups interested in my affairs?"

He was getting into a two-piece cazsuit when the door of the bedroom, unexpectedly, opened.

Before it had swung all the way he had dived to his kitbag, extracted a stungun and gotten it aimed at the doorway.

"Are you still miffed about last night?" inquired Tessie.

Uninvited, she rolled a waist-high canister-shaped piece of equipment across his threshold.

"Your voice's changed," he observed.

The young woman was wearing a simple one-piece slaxsuit and had her long seablue hair tied back with a kelp-colored strand of ribbon. "This is me is why," she explained. "The genuine Tessie Stardrake."

"But the SOF terminal and monitors are still resting up inside your coco." He tapped his own temple.

"They're not even so much as peeking. Really." She crossed her hearts.

Sand seamed up his suit. "How'd you manage to get in?"

"Oh, I used a handpick. Duplicates any fingerprints. Very useful."

"I don't like the idea of you guys breaking into my digs whenever—"

"John, they're not here. Honest. This is only me."

She tried a smile while pushing the gadget nearer to his jellobed. "Anyway, are you ready for the briefing?"

Sand watched her. "That's a portable briefing unit?"

"Exactly."

"Awful dinky, and it's got dents all over its side there."

"Actually it's space-war surplus, picked up in an Army & Navy satellite thriftshop orbiting—"

"Go ahead, let's get going."

She was watching him with her pretty blue head cocked slightly to the left. "You aren't very cordial this—"

"Did you slip a bug under my bed last night?"

Her blue eyes went wide. "Whatever makes you think that?"

"Mostly the fact that I found one there."

"Well, gee, I have no recollection of it," she said, frowning. "Although I maybe might've done it while under SOF, Inc control. In which case I—"

"Never mind."

"I really wish you'd try to think of me as a person, an individual. The way you did when first we met in—"

"I don't like agents." He settled into a sling chair. "That's why I freelance and never associate with anybody in the profession."

"Listen, I don't much care for all this espionage and counterespionage stuff, or even simple missing persons capers," she confided, sitting opposite him. "As for disliking secret agents and private operatives . . . you should've seen my ex-husbands. What a pair. Both were sixteen years my senior and—"

"Let's have the briefing."

"But what did I know back when I wed them? Raised in the Sacred Convent of Our Doublejointed Lady of—"

"Tessie, we've gone beyond the personal revelations stage."

"Phil and Will were their names. That should've been the old tipoff." She sighed and three of her four breasts shivered beneath her tunic. "Did you ever try to murmur, 'I love you, Phil. I love you, Will?' No zing." She reached into her shoulder bag. "I'll just check out the instruction manual for this—"

"Don't you even know how to run the damn thing?"

"Not this particular model, no." The thin manual looked to be printed on real papersub and it had a large ragged hole perforating all the pages.

"Why the hole?"

"I told you it was war surplus. Let's see now . . . um . . . activate switch marked ON. That sounds simple enough."

Leaving his chair, Sand crouched beside the machine. "This is just a condensed version of the standard Briefer Unit." He flipped three toggles, pushed two buttons, turned a crank. "There."

By the time he was seated again the compact briefing unit was humming and projecting a two foot by two foot rectangle of light on the nearest wall.

Tessie rubbed at her blue nose. "Ought it to be giving off that burning feathers smell?"

Sand swung out one bare foot, booting the machine.

It hopped once and then the tiny swirls of greenish smoke ceased wisping out from its underside.

On the rectangle appeared a still photo of a slim chestnut-haired girl of about thirteen. She was smiling, but there was a sadness in her thin freckled face.

"This is Brandywine, Julia Marie," intoned the deep rumbling voice that came out of one side of the portable briefer. "Female, age thirteen (ESC) at the time this portrait was taken, of the Earth Humanoid class. Only child of Jonah and Hazel Brandywine, notorious traitors and—"

"There hasn't been time to update all of this," put in Tessie in a whisper.

"Was she altered after this?" asked Sand. "That was standard procedure with kids of convicted spies and killers back eight ten years ago."

"The Esmeraldan government gave her a conventional brainwipe," answered the machine. "As well as an identity transformation. Nothing unusual. She wasn't changed physically at all, but of course she has no idea who she really is."

"You've got ID stuff on her?" Sand was leaning forward, staring at the image of the lost girl.

"Fingerprints, retprints, voxprints, brainscans, medfax readout," said the voice of the briefer. "The works." After it had whirred for about ten seconds a plazsealed packet came easing out of a slot in its back.

The packet hit the thermorug.

Sand, still watching the image of the girl, didn't pick the thing up. "What was the new name they hung on her?"

"Jill Gaynes."

"What about the foster parents?"

"Don and Maggie Kilmartin," replied the briefer unit. "Residents of the planet Murdstone. Pictures coming up."

The Kilmartins were humanoid, plump. They looked amiable and pleasant and like the sort of folks Sand always avoided.

"Mr. Kilmartin ran a fairly successful computer software boutique until some five years ago," continued the machine. "Then a foolish fling with a young lady in the wholesale floppydisc trade caused the breakup of his heretofor happy marriage as well as the complete and total collapse of his small business empire. How often does one encounter such middle-aged follies in the course of—"

"What happened to Jill?" prodded Sand.

"After the ruin of both the Kilmartin business and menage, Jill lived on a few months with Mrs. Kilmartin, who'd become a hopeless food additive junkie due to her sorrows. She had, so it is reliably rumored, a $500 a day MSG habit ... At any rate, Jill was sent out to the Hellquad planet of Fazenda. Which we see in our next slide."

A longshot of a bright green stretch of woodland flashed onto the wall.

"That doesn't look all that pestilential," commented Tessie.

"Nothing looks bad at that distance," said Sand, slouching in his seat.

"The girl in question," resumed the machine, "was residing with an aunt of the ill-fated Mrs. Kilmartin. Her name is Molly Yronsyde."

A thickset woman of about fifty appeared now. Her frazzled hair was an unbelievable shade of red. She wore a one-piece mansuit, carried a whip.

"The whip was used only on cattle, so far as we've been able to determine," explained the briefer. "Grouts, cows, snergs, etc."

"That's the business she's in, cattle?"

"Mrs. Yronsyde, a widow for these past eleven years by the bye, is a formidable agribiz tycoon on Fazenda. She owns and operates a farm that covers 8500 acres."

"Lot of land," said Tessie.

"Jill's no longer living with her?"

"Indications are the girl hasn't been seen on the ranch for at least two and one half years."

"Could she have died there?"

"We have no data."

"What does Yronsyde say?"

"We don't know, since four, possibly five, of our previous SOF agents expired, in one violent way or the other, while trying to arrange interviews with Mrs. Y."

"She cause the violence?"

"There's no proof."

"Interesting string of coincidences, though." Sand slouched deeper, gazing up at the domed ceiling. "Anything else?"

"Picture of Jonas and Hazel Brandywine."

This was a prison shot with the couple standing in front of a blank gray wall. Hazel was thin, vaguely pretty. Jonas was a tall, gaunt man whose hair was already thinning. Their daughter didn't look much like either of them.

"Since they've been in a suspended state," mentioned the machine, "they have remained thirty-five and thirty-nine respectively. One wonders at their initial reactions to this paradox of—"

"Got any other facts?"

"That's the lot."

Sand said, "I want pictures, along with background packets, on the other five guys who tackled this business ahead of me. Plus as much as SOF has on what they did on Fazenda before expiring."

"We don't like to give out that sort of—"

"But you will."

After a few seconds of silence the briefer said, "We'll have the material to you by nightfall."

"Thanks." Sand grinned, patting the canister on its top.

Chapter 3

It was always bright midday down in Mallcity 3.

Sand stepped out of a droptube early that evening.

There was noise as well as light down here several hundred feet below the capital city of Barnum's major territory. Music, laughter, sales pitches came spilling out of dozens of shops and eateries.

Dodging a gaggle of green-toned tourists bedecked with cameras, Sand headed for Ramp 9. He hurried by a stungunsmith's shop, a cyborg accessories store with a display window filled with glittering false arms, a Porno Shack and a Dizzy Dumas Home Computer Discount Warehouse. In front of this latter a plump birdman was arguing with a yellow-suited humanoid salesman and blocking the way.

". . . as I suspected. A flimflam," the birdman was accusing, waving the sheaf of papers he held in his feathered fist.

"Sir, Dizzy Dumas stands by its integrity and—"

"Sez you! Right there in the window you state 'DIZZY WILL MATCH ANY PRICE!' Am I right?"

"Certainly, sir, Dizzy Dumas can't be undersold."

"Okay, so here I am showing you the price the Plaut Home Cookin' Database goes for at one of your competitors'. $26.50."

"Impossible, sir. The lowest price in the known universe is $65.99. Not including the Aroma Attachment."

"Hocky! Look, see this? $26.50." He fluttered a catalog in the salesman's perspiring face, causing three green feathers to fall free of his thick wrist. "There it is in black, white and fuchsia."

"Where is this dadratted place?" The salesman grabbed the catalog, scanned the bright cover. "Parallel World 6A? I never heard of any—"

"I been trying to tell you." The birdman unfolded a chart. "You take this celestial course and right exactly here ... see where I'm pointing with my talon? ... you make a spacetime jump across to the—"

"I don't think parallel worlds count."

"Then Dizzy *can* be undersold?"

"No, never, but . . ."

Sand edged around the two, continued on his way. He sprinted up a side ramp and arrived at a licorice-tinted glazdoor. *Your Humble Servant Enterprises* was etched discreetly near the handle.

The door anticipated him, whispered open.

"Ooh lala!" greeted a perky petite android maid with a skimpy black frock and a frilly white cap. " 'ow may Fifi serve you, Monzoor?"

"Where's Cookie?"

Her nose wrinkled, her slim shoulders shrugged. "That one? Why do you wish 'im?"

"Business."

Fifi shrugged again. "Zee backroom."

Nodding, Sand made his way through the butlers, valets, grooms, chefs and assorted other andy servants gathered in the Your Humble Servant showroom.

Cookie Rensie was a chubby dog-faced man, wearing a tight-fitting tuxsuit. He was sitting in a snug glazchair, facing a small floating glaztable. Atop the table was an open box of dog biscuits. "Ever been on a diet, Sand?"

"Nope."

Cookie dipped a paw into the box and brought out a greenish biscuit of a bone shape. "Broccoli flavor," he said forlornly. "It's enough to give a man the wimwams."

"My order ready?"

The dog-faced store manager took a dispirited bite of the biscuit. "Doing the prudent thing is never any fun," he observed. "For breakfast I'm allowed two oatmeal biscuits, lunch is one lone cottage cheese biscuit. Ah, how I've fallen. Used to start the day with something like a grout haunch smothered with buttersub sauce and washed down with a flagon of mead that had a couple of whiffen eggs whipped up in it. Then a tureen of puffed pigsfeet soup and a side order of whipped cream with—"

"No use dwelling on the past," advised Sand, stepping over the torso of a defunct servitor android and stopping next to Cookie's table. "My order?"

Cookie waved a lax paw in the direction of the workroom on his left. "Yes, all set to go," he said as he took another mournful bite. "Oh, excuse me for not offering you a biscuit."

"Thanks all the same, but no." He headed for the workroom doorway. "Does he look natural on the outside?"

"Yes, exactly as you stipulated." Cookie came sighing up out of his chair. "Did you ever feel you were in a horrible, dreary rut?"

"Nope."

"Day in day out it's nothing but these awful machines. Butlers, maids, chefs. Chefs, butlers, maids. 'Oui, monzoor' 'Lunch will be served promptly at noon.' 'Your smoking jacket, sahib.' Lordy me, it's enough to—"

"That's him?" Sand was in the storeroom, pointing a thumb at a brand new butler-valet android.

The figure was tall, lean and built to resemble a human of about fifty. He had a sharp-featured face, dominated by a disdainful nose. He was dressed in a conservative three-piece bizsuit of a somber color.

"The name they have seen fit to bestow upon me, sir, is Munson," spoke the android, with a very slight nod in Sand's direction. "If you will permit me, I shall mention now that I consider it an extremely loathsome appellation and mention it never again. Munson at your service, sir." He bowed. "Might I mention that your strenuous life is starting to take its toll? Traces of pouches forming 'neath the eyes, a bit of—"

"How come he's so salty?" Sand asked of the dog-faced man.

"All the Munsons are. Want me to read you the specifications out of the manual or show you some schematics?"

"No need," decided Sand as he took a couple steps back from Munson and eyed him.

"The master has a fondness for, one notes, blue-heads." The android reached out a white-gloved hand, removed a blue hair from Sand's tunic, sneered at it before allowing it to drift to the plazplank floor. "Ah, well, one must be prepared for all sorts of lewd and—"

"The lady in question is remaining on Barnum,"

said Sand. "While you and I, Munson old chum, will be journeying out to the Hellquad planets."

"Oh, so?" The believable left eyebrow rose a fraction. "One hears that those four planets are the sinkhole of the universe."

"One hears correctly. Although sinkhole may be too optimistic a word."

Munson bowed faintly. "Allow me to say, sir, that I consider it my duty to follow and serve. I never allow myself to voice even the mildest criticism of such dippy plans. Nay, wither you go blundering, there also follow I."

"He's got the extra stuff built in, Cookie?"

Cookie finished off his broccoli dog biscuit. "Just like you ordered," he answered, swallowing. "All cleverly concealed not only to fool the opposition but to confound any and all customs officials."

"I do hope," said Munson, "if I may be so bold as to express a concern which has been gnawing at my vitals, we shall not be engaged in anything of an unlawful nature."

"Out in the Hellquad, there's just about nothing that's illegal," Sand said. "But, you can put your mind at ease, we're on the side of law and order."

"That takes a considerable weight off one's mind." Munson allowed himself a very brief sigh of relief.

"Gather up your gear, Munson, and let's depart."

"Where to, sir, if I may inquire?"

"I have to meet someone over on Ramp 27," replied Sand. "Do you think you can stand discreetly by while I dine?"

"Yes, to be sure," said the android. "One does that exceedingly well, if one may be so immodest as to so state."

• • •

The smell of oregano, tomato sauce and melted cheese was heavy in the air. Up on the small pedestal stage at the center of the restaurant a halfsize android replica of Thomas Carlyle stood reciting.

". . . whatever gods or fetishes a man may have about him, and pay tithes to," the android was saying, "and mumble prayers to, the real 'religion' that is in him is his *practical Hero-worship* . . ."

"Guess you're really enjoying this," said the small bald man sitting across the table from Sand.

"Not especially, Hack."

Hack O'Hara's head bobbed once. "Sorry. I figured with you being a 19th Century Earth Lit buff that you'd get a boot out of dining at the Eminent Victorians Pizza Theater."

"It's 19th century Earth fiction I dote on," explained Sand, picking up another wedge of his mushroom and seaweed pizza. "Novels."

Hack tapped the menu. "None of these bozos scheduled to do a turn tonight is a novelist, huh? John Henry Newman, Herbert Spencer, Edward Whymper, James Anthony Froude, Queen Victoria?"

"Nary a one."

"Sorry." Shrugging, Hack closed the menu. "By the way, you haven't commented on my appearance."

"Thought it best not to."

"You think, huh, I look like a schlepp?"

"Liked you better with hair."

"I decided the hairpiece was an affectation," confided Hack. "I don't look at my best with a cabeza covered with blond ringlets. Emmy Lou agreed, during the all too brief time we shared a love nest in—"

"Hack."

"Hum?"

"Of late everybody seems bent on telling me his personal troubles. Don't join the throng."

"Sorry." He glanced over at the platform. "Who's this new gink?"

"Matthew Arnold. I'd like to hire you, Hack."

"No, sorry, no." His bald head flashed and flickered in the subdued orange light as he shook it negatively and vigorously from side to side. "Do you know how many different ways they can punch your ticket out in the Hellquad planets or—"

"How'd you know where I was heading?"

"I find things out," answered Hack. "Fact is, I can't help myself. This great gift of mine, this psi power, just naturally makes me a natural data-tapper. Alls I do is start thinking about you, got to wondering what you were up to and if maybe you were working for SOF again . . . wellsir, zam! My mind was roaming through the top secret bowels of the local branch of Soldiers of Fortune, Inc. There was this stuff about you, fresh added only today." He spread his hands wide.

"Did you notice anything else while your mind was on the prowl?"

"You been putting the boots to a nifty-looking bluehead but not one set but two of exceptional—"

"Notice anyone else trying to tap, any sign there'd been siphoning done?"

"That's tricky to spot, John. Takes more time and . . . a little money."

Sand ate at the pizza for a moment. "I'll pay you $5000."

"Trubux or local?"

"Trudollars."

"Not if I have to go to the Hellquad. Five thousand wouldn't tempt me to commit suicide that way."

"You don't have to go near any of the Hellquad planets," promised Sand.

"Okay, it's a deal. What do you need?"

"I'm looking for a girl named Jill Gaynes."

"Sure, I know. She's the . . ." He lowered his voice. "The Brandywine kid. Last seen on Fazenda. I read up on that when I was finding out about you."

"Okay, first off I want you to find out who else here on Barnum is interested in the girl," said Sand, wiping his fingers on his checkered neocloth napkin. "Who's been tapping SOF, what government agencies are interested, what they're doing about it."

"And who's been knocking off those other SOF ginks?"

"That's something I hope to find out, yep," answered Sand. "Soon as you learn anything, send me a report, using the usual scramble code we worked out. I'll be at the Sheridan-Ritz on Fazenda."

"Hey, that's the best hotel on the planet," said Hack admiringly. "I was reading a travel bureau computer's database just the other day, for lack of anything better to—"

"After you get everything you can out of the computers here on Barnum, go to Esmeralda."

Hack rubbed his hairless head, then his stomach. "I get space sick pretty easy, John. Which is probably why I've stuck close to home and never exploited my marvelous gift for info siphoning to its fullest extent. I often think that if I had your nerve I'd be a—"

"I'll add a $2500 travel bonus."

"Um . . . well . . . okay I guess."

"On Esmeralda, Hack, dig into the whole damn Brandywine case," instructed Sand. "Get me all you can about the couple and their daughter. I want stuff on how she was processed, who did the new ID implanting and so on. Turn up whatever you can on this Kilmartin family that took her in after her folks were executed. Make a side trip to Murdstone if you have to."

"Yet another space trip?"

"I'll throw in $1000 more."

"Sure, okay. I suppose I really can't exploit my marvelous gift to its fullest if I'm a stay-at-home all—"

"Also find out everything you can about how and why the Brandywines have come back to life."

"You think there's something not kosher about the deal?"

"I think it's odd and strange that five SOF agents have gotten themselves killed in the few days since it was announced the Brandywines would be coming back to life."

"Somebody doesn't want the kid found, huh?"

"Maybe."

Hack folded his hands atop the table, glanced over at the Queen Victoria halfsize simulacrum on the stage. "We're longtime buddies, right?"

"Yep."

"Then you won't be ticked or perturbed if I ask for half my fee in front, huh? Sorry to sound negative, John, but . . . well, lots of people who've been going out to the Hellquad of late haven't come back."

"I'll give you the whole and entire $8500," said Sand, grinning. "No use your having to bother my estate for it."

"I know you'll survive, you always have, but—"

"You'll get the money tomorrow morning before I take off."

"Leaving tomorrow morning, huh? That's very soon," said Hack. "Much too soon to my way of thinking."

Chapter
4

Sand was stroking his chin when he returned to his space-time liner cabin.

"May one inquire as to the reason for your pensiveness, sir?" Munson, wearing a sewdosilk lounging robe occupied one of the lemon-hued room's two sprawl chairs. Arranged on the plaz table in front of him was an assortment of travel brochures and pamphlets.

"Been thinking." Sand crossed to the desk alcove, slid the passenger list he'd just acquired from the Chief Robosteward out of his tunic pocket and spread it out on the desk top.

"So have I," said the android butler-valet. "My own cogitations were prompted by a quick perusal of this assortment of gaudy literature provided free of charge by the Spazhopps organization to those of us who can afford to travel First Class."

"Uh huh." Sand sat with his back to the mechanical man.

"I was, for instance, moderately unsettled by this leaflet entitled *The 99 Social Diseases You're Most Likely To Contract On The Hellquad Planets & How To Cope With Them*," began Munson. "I am myself immune to all of them save Reisberson's Dork Rust and hernia of the gudgeon, but you, sir, especially in light of your proclivities, may well pick up fifty or sixty of these dreadful maladies in the course of our—"

"I've had shots." Sand checked several names on the list.

"Ah, but such vicious ills as Harrison's Technicolor Herpes are actually made worse by medication."

"Harrison's Technicolor Herpes only develops as a result of sex between two consenting wolfmen with the mange."

"In most cases, but—"

"Hush up," advised Sand, hunching his shoulders as he continued his study.

"Let us then consider this other brochure. The title is *101 Vile Things To Do On Fazenda* and there is also a special supplement devoted to *50 More Beastly & Rotten Pastimes*," said Munson. "One was especially struck by the note of caution which serves as an epigraph of sorts. May I quote, sir?"

"In a low, faint voice."

"Ahum. 'DIRE WARNING! Yes, Fazenda is a swell place for FUNSEEKING tourists such as yourself to do dozens of delightful VILE and DISGUSTING things. REMEMBER, though, that it is also the SINKHOLE of the universe . . .' Perhaps you recall my passing a similar judgment. But to continue. 'NEVER for any reason stray beyond the clearly marked SAFE ZONES in whatever low city you visit. It's worth your very LIFE to do so!' "

"It's unlikely we're going to find the girl in a Safe Zone."

"Then we'll be risking life and—"

"Probably, yes."

"It seems, if I may be so bold as to point out the fact, foolhardy."

"It is," agreed Sand, turning to face the android. "Which is the main reason the work pays so damn well."

Munson sighed. "One fears it is pointless to pursue the subject. I shall, therefore, forgo quoting from the warning appended to *The Top-Rated Fleshpots, Low Dives, Thieves' Dens and Hellholes of Fazenda*."

"Be a waste of time." He picked the list from the desk. "Did you check out the cabin?"

"Of course, sir, making use of the detecting gadget you caused to be built into my humble carcass."

"And?"

Brushing some of the pamphlets aside, Munson picked up a minibug between gloved thumb and forefinger. "This was rather ineptly concealed beneath this very chair upon which I repose."

"Toss it over."

The android valet obliged. "Of Barnum origin."

"Yeah, it is." Sand bounced it in the palm of his hand a few times, then spread the passenger list out on his lap. "I note several candidates for the role of planter."

"How, may I venture to ask, did you persuade the purser to turn over a copy, sir?"

"Used a parasite-control disc on his conk," replied Sand. "Lot easier than trying to con or bribe him."

"The crew mechanisms, from the brief yet sufficient gander one got while coming aboard at the spaceport, are of inferior make," said Munson. "But then they can't all be Munsons."

Sand said, "Several spurious sounding names on the First Class and Second Class lists. We'll look into them all later."

"I admire your ability to sort the wheat from the chaff, sir, or, in this instance, the chaff from the wheat," said the android. "To me almost all names sound dubious. I much prefer numbers."

Tapping the list, Sand said, "There's also a source of trouble traveling under her own name."

"Not, one fervently hopes, another young lady for you to become romantically involved with."

"I intend to avoid this lady like all ninety-nine of Fazenda's favorite social diseases. She's a reporter name of Glory Forbes."

"You have had encounters with her prior to this?"

"Run-ins. Last time was a year ago, out on Barafunda. I was working on that teleportation kidnapping of the Grand Vizier's entire harem."

"An attractive person, is she?"

"She is," admitted Sand. "Glory is also a persistent, aggressive, salty lady who'll stop at nothing to get a story for that damn *Galactic Enquirer* magazine she works for. I have met feisty redheads before, but she—"

"Ah," exclaimed the valet, sitting suddenly upright. "Um."

"What?" Sand eyed him. "You having a malfunction?"

"An insight rather, sir." He rose up, smoothed his lounging robe and went striding to the lemonyellow door of the nearest wardrobe closet. "That explains who this person I caught snooping is."

When he opened the door, the body of a pretty redhead came toppling out.

Chapter
5

Sand lifted the fallen young woman up and arranged her in one of the chairs. "What'd you use on her?"

Peeling the glove from his left hand, Munson held up his forefinger. "This, sir," he replied. "The concealed stungun you ordered built into my—"

"Okay, then she shouldn't be out for more than an hour." Sand stepped back from her chair. "When'd you shoot her?"

"One senses a note of reprobation." He slipped his glove, slowly, back on. "My operational assumption, sir, has been that you had these many weapons and gadgets added to my basic persona so that I might utilize them as I saw fit. Yet when I return to our cabin to find this young woman snooping and—"

"I've been hoping to pass as an idle playboy, bound for some vile fun out in the Hellquads and accompanied by his devoted servant. Rather than pack weapons, bugging devices and the like in a steamer trunk I paid

Your Humble Servant to convert you into a walking arsenal."

"Only too glad to serve in any manner that—"

"Thing is, Munson, this is Glory Forbes you've zonked here," said Sand. "That indicates I'm not going to be able to pass as a pleasure-bent wastrel anymore. On top of which, Glory and I weren't on very cordial terms even before you stunned her."

"Might one suggest you look on the bright side?" He held up his left hand. "Suppose I had, impulsively, used my disintegrator finger rather than—"

"You're right, things could be worse." Sand stroked his chin. "And maybe we can dump her back in her own cabin before she comes to, use a simple local brainwipe on her and fix it so she won't—"

"Like heck you will, Sand." Glory Forbes sat up, shook her head, frowned up at him. She was an assertive young woman in her early twenties.

"Hi, Glory. Nice meeting you again." He backed farther off from her.

She nodded at the android. "What's the name of your mechanical pansy? Want to make sure the Enquirer attorneys get it right when we sue your toke off." She brushed at her long red hair with one hand.

"C'mon, you're not going to sue anyone," Sand told her. "I've got you on breaking and entering. Maybe we'll throw in intended assault, invasion of privacy and—"

"Might we add defamation of character?" suggested Munson. "To suggest that my masculinity is not—"

"Smuggling weapons onto a Controlled Planet," said Glory, tossing her head. "That charge I'll take to the Space Code Authority." She leaned back, smoothing down the short skirt of her two-piece bizsuit. "Maybe I'll add sexual assault while stunned, which carries an automatic ten year (ESC) sentence when committed in space, and intent to sell into white slavery to my own list of charges against—"

"No rational white slaver would buy you, Glory. They're all astute businessmen and they know you'd bring them only grief and eventual ruin should they—"

"Tell you what." She smiled, briefly, up at him. "Let's see if maybe we can work out a compromise."

"I'd rather be sued."

"Send this nitwit gadget away, we'll talk."

"Miss, it is my solemn duty," Munson informed her, "according to the basic laws of robotics, to stand by my employer at all times and see that no danger befalls him. One would be shirking one's duty were one to leave him alone with the likes of—"

"Hooey," remarked Glory, standing up. "Sand and I are . . . oops." She swayed, legs going slack, almost fell.

Sand lunged and caught her. "Easy now."

"Permanent damage to my balance center," she said. "We'll add that to the bill of particulars. Ought to net me about two million trudollars when my—"

"Acting too feisty right after being stunned is all that's wrong with you." He deposited her, gently, back in the slouch chair. "Sit for a spell. Munson, step into the hall."

"Is this wise, sir? The lady seems fully capable, in spite of her present wobbly condition, of doing you serious bodily and psychological harm."

"I'll risk it. Go."

"To hear is, alas, to obey." The android moved to the door. "You have but to scream out in agony, sir, and I'll rush back inside."

Glory watched Munson exit. "He's very thoughtful."

"Okay." Sand sat in the other chair, facing the

redhead. "What kind of shady deal do you have in mind, Glory?"

She slumped slightly. "Boy, I haven't been stunned in near a year, not since the grout herders' sitdown strike out on Murdstone," she said. "That time they used a cattlestunner and it—"

"Munson is a shade overzealous. There was no need to stun you."

"Thanks."

"A simple bop on the skull would've sufficed. What do you want?"

"You're going to Fazenda."

"Along with everybody else on this damn liner, sure."

"So am I."

"Figured as much."

"You don't like me."

"True again."

"I don't much care for you."

Sand nodded. "A situation that's not likely to change much on either side."

"It's too bad in a way. Visually you're an attractive guy," she said. "You're kind of like that andy of yours. A slick surface, but all sorts of junk and deadly devices concealed inside."

'You're attractive, too," said Sand, watching her. "What makes you loathsome, though, is your damn dedication to your tacky profession. If you weren't such a fanatic about—"

"I think we've pretty well established the point that we can't stand each other," cut in the red-haired reporter. "Even so, Sand, I'd like to make a suggestion to you. You're going to Fazenda on the Brandywine business and so am I."

"Brandywine?"

"Drop it, you ceased to be able to look guileless long ago," she said. "You want to find the missing daughter, so do I."

"That makes us competitors."

"No, you want her for SOF's clients, I simply want an exclusive interview with the kid."

"Not a kid, Glory. She'll be about your age, and after eight years out in the Hellquads I doubt she's any too innocent."

"I don't care if she's turning tricks in a toadmen's flophouse. We want her story, the sleazier the better."

"I don't like to collaborate. Fact is, I won't."

"This is an unusual situation. A very rough and wild planet, lots of hazards to watch out for," Glory said. "You and I are pretty shrewd, Sand, we'll complement each other on this."

"Nope."

"Better to have me on your side than working against you," she warned him with a faint smile.

He returned her smile with a bleak grin. "Don't try to screw me up in any way, Glory," he said quietly.

She stood up, steady on her feet now. "One of the things about me you don't yet fully understand," she said, "is that when I set out to foul you up, you never know about it until it's happened. And that's much too late. Bye, Sand."

He stayed in his chair and she let herself out of the cabin.

Chapter
6

The catman cabbie yowled with fright, orangish fur bristling at his uniform collar. "I knew I shouldn't of did this foolhardy thing," he said as their landcab shuddered again and then came to a thumping, rattling stop in the middle of the rutted street. "You appealed to the sportsman in me, get me? Drive us away from the spaceport, ditch any tail. A challenge, know what I mean?"

There were ruined gutted buildings looming up all around them. Towering ruins of glaz, plaz, neowood and sewdo steel. Dangling from a rusty lamppost that tilted far over was a pitted, battered sign announcing: *Street Gang Reservation #11. Not a SAFE ZONE. Travel At Your Own Risk.*

"Engine trouble?" asked Sand from the backseat.

"We're doomed, mister," the driver said, starting to quiver. "Engine's gone and conked with us stuck in the middle of a government gangland. Look! Look!" He pointed a paw at one of the decayed tenements. "They're starting to come slinking out of their foul lairs."

"Might one suggest," said Munson, "that you set about repairing this vehicle, my good man?"

"Are you goofy? I'd have to get outside the cab to lift the damn hood, wouldn't I?" The cabbie shook his shaggy head. "I got a wife and kiddies and several penpals all over the universe."

Six lizard youths in one-piece orange fightsuits were drifting along the cracked, littered street. Talons snapping, dark glasses catching the rays of the hot afternoon sun.

"Do you see what that big lunk with the obscene tattoo is toting?" cried the driver. "It's a portable barbeque. Gor, they're going to cook us alive."

"I am certain they would slaughter you first, then pluck and clean you," mentioned Munson helpfully. "You would be dead and gone long before the cooking occurred."

Sand nudged the android. "Fix this crate."

"Me? My duties surely do not include automotive—"

"Yep, I had that knack added to your basic abilities. C'mon, move."

Sighing, the valet eased out of the stranded cab. "Is one free to dispatch these hooligans who are fast approaching us, sir?"

"Just stun them, stack them on the curb."

"Close the blinking door!" urged the shivering cabbie. "They'll jump in and slaughter us."

Munson obliged, then strolled to the front of the cab and, disdainfully, lifted the hood.

"Hey, you frapping nurf, don't you know this is Flamboyant Reptilian Avengers territory?"

"Begone," suggested the android as he stared at the vehicle's inner workings.

The six gang members halted a few feet from the cab.

Sand glanced out the rear window. At least there was no sign of anyone following them. He'd succeeded in ditching Glory Forbes. Too bad in a way, since she was an attractive young—

"Yikes!" yelled the driver. "Another pack of them coming up at nine o'clock. Looks like the Sylvan Parkway Disembowelers."

Sand looked to his left, saw five large shaggy apelads in seagreen two-piece kilsuits clumping out of a rubble-filled alley and coming for his halted cab.

"Worse than the Avengers, are they?"

The driver removed his cap, put his paws together. "Dear Kali, I beseech you to let me die an easeful death."

"That bad, huh?"

"One hesitates to discomfort the entire sorry lot of you," Munson was saying to the lizard gang as he fiddled with the engine.

The lizard with the cooking gear inched closer. "We gonna slice off yer goonies," he threatened. "Then we gonna whack off yer nixon and—"

"Shoo." Munson emerged from under the hood.

"Aw, this nurf's a flaming figbar," accused another of the gang. "That's disgusting."

"Were I truly convinced I was disgusting enough to disgust you, young man, I would indeed be downcast." The android stroked off his lefthand glove. "Well, will you depart quietly?"

"We gonna warp yer dinkens!"

"Yeah! Let's cook this figgie!"

"Youse said it!"

Zzzzzzummmmm!

A thin sizzling line of purplish light shot out of the

android's extended forefinger. It hit the chest of the nearest green Avenger.

"Mudder!" he gasped, scaly hands clutching at his middle. He spun in a lazy lopsided way before falling to the street atop a dead goat.

"Did youse lamp that?"

"Frapped Kevin with nothing but his finger."

"You better watch out, figgie."

"Take flight," Munson advised them.

"Naw, we gonna avenge our fallen brudder. That's what we specializes in, hence our name."

Zzzzzummmmmm!

Zzzzzzummmmmm!

Two more Avengers dropped, stunned, to the street.

"Rowr," announced a Disemboweler.

The quintet of surly apes was drawing close to the disabled cab.

"Bless Bess," sighed Munson, "another batch of louts."

The apparent leader of the Disembowelers snarled at the android, thumped at his broad shaggy chest with both paws. "Rowr, growrr," he said.

"Oh, so?" Munson pointed his forefinger at him. "I really have absolutely no more time for this nonsense, young fellows."

Zzzzzummmmmm!

The head ape did a hop into the fuzzy afternoon air when the stunbeam hit him. He came down on his heels, teetered, staggered backward, fell over.

His associates gathered around him, staring down.

Munson returned his attentions to repairing the engine.

He fixed it in less than ten minutes and by the time he climbed back into the cab next to Sand every remaining gang member had long since departed.

"I do hope all this violence will not have a permanent effect on my character," he said, rubbing his smudged glove fingertips together.

"Excessively quaint," remarked Munson, who was perched on the edge of a frail canebottom chair. "At least to my tastes."

"That's why the White Pickets Hometel is a good place to lie low." Sand had the android's jacket rolled up to expose his metallic right side. He punched a number pattern out on the series of tiny buttons thereon and a narrow strip of faxpaper came ribboning out. "Something from Hack O'Hara coming through already."

"Might not your adversaries, including the formidable Miss Forbes, see through such a flimsy subterfuge?" inquired Munson while his inner workings printed out the information that had been sent on from the planet Barnum by O'Hara. "Sand thinks we think he would not reside in a hotel with chintz covers on each and every piece of furniture, lace doilies beneath myriad ugly vases, strawberry pattern cafe curtains on all the windows, cloying embroidered maxims hanging on the wallpapered walls. Therefore, that shall be the first place we will hunt for him."

Tearing off the long strip of paper, Sand covered the mechanical man's side. "There are a lot of quaint hotels, motels and hometels in this area," he reminded. "We registered under false names and, using your builtin hypobeam, we also fixed the clerk so he thinks he registered two chubby birdmen from Alpha Centauri who travel in the gourmet scratch feed line."

"Perhaps we are safe for a time," conceded the android. "Perhaps we are not." He rose. "Would you care for a cup of tea, sir?"

"Nope." He settled into a chintz-covered rocker.

"Perhaps a mug of cocoa? Since we have a quaint kitchen attached to our suite, one feels obliged to—"

"Nothing just now, except silence."

Munson reseated himself. "The samplers on yonder wall are simpleminded even for a planet as low on the scale as this one," he observed. " 'I Never Met A Snurf I Didn't Like,' 'It Takes A Heap Of Gribblin' To Make A House A—' "

"Quiet." Sand was skimming the encoded message from O'Hara.

"Has your tapper chum passed on anything of interest?"

"Several things."

"Such as?"

"At least two separate groups succeeded in tapping SOF's computers and communications system on Barnum," replied Sand. "Hack hasn't identified one, but the other is the Political Espionage Office."

"The PEO, eh? The efficient and rather ruthless intelligence and counterintelligence arm of the Barnum System government."

"The same, and their interest in Soldiers of Fortune, Inc's central headquarters didn't commence until the day after the Brandywines' attorney first contacted the SOF field office on Esmeralda."

"Suggesting that PEO is interested in the exonerated spy couple and their wayward offspring."

"Yep." Sand nodded. "Using his psi-based tapping ability, Hack nosed around in PEO's files. They've got more safeguards than SOF, blocks that keep out even a wild talent like Hack. Even so, he did learn that part of the PEO interest is because of a gent named Dr. Hugo Gobblinn."

"Known in scientific and military circles as the Father of Death 1," said the android. "As well as the Father of Death 2, Death 3, Death—"

"Chemical-biological weapons all the way up to Death 6," cut in Sand. "Gobblinn met his own end in a nasty skytram crash just about the time the Brandywines were arrested back ten or so years ago. Unfortunately, from a military point of view, there wasn't enough left of him to patch together."

"All for the best, since the vicious sort of weapons fathered by that—"

"Point is, he maybe perfected Death 7." Sand leaned back in the rocker, and it creaked. "Rumored to be more deadly than Deaths 1–6 put together. No records or notes were found in Gobblinn's effects, and it was assumed at the time that he'd never completed his work on the project."

Munson steepled his fingers. "Were not the Brandywines convicted of stealing secrets from this selfsame Doctor Gobblinn?"

"They were, but only stuff pertaining to Death 6," he said. "It appears the PEO thinks now that they not only aren't innocent, but that they know something about Death 7 as well."

"And the secret of this Death 7 has, obviously, not surfaced in all the intervening years?"

"It hasn't, no. But it's possible the Brandywines really are spies and traitors and they managed to steal all of Dr. Hugo Gobblinn's papers on Death 7."

"Could it be, may one suggest, that the missing daughter might be privy to where the secret is hidden?"

"That would sure as hell explain why the PEO is interested in Julia Brandywine and who's hunting for her." Sand left the rocker. "Might even explain why the Brandywines were resurrected."

"So that they could lead the Political Espionage Office to the secret of Death 7."

"Death 7, whatever it is exactly, would come in handy right now with several new wars in the offing in the Barnum System and beyond."

The android shook his head. "Should your promise have any validity, and I am inclined to venture that it does, our position is even more dire than we originally were led to believe. Not only do we have to cope with the abundant snares and pitfalls of this dreary planet, but we will be called upon to dodge and outwit sundry spies, secret agents and weaponsmongers who are seeking the secret of Death 7."

"You're right, Munson," said Sand, grinning. "Remind me to ask for a bonus."

"What of your predecessors? Did this O'Hara person convey any—"

"Four out of the five contacted an SOF field agent here on Fazenda soon after arriving," replied Sand, pacing on the flowered rug. "I think I'll approach the fellow myself, but obliquely."

"Shall I accompany you into the mean streets of—"

"Stick here; monitor anything else that comes in from Hack," said Sand as he moved to the door. "This I'll tackle alone."

"Very good, sir. Perhaps I shall putter in our cozy kitchen while you are out and about."

"Putter away." Sand left.

Chapter
7

The golden-haired little waif in the pathetically tattered plyodress gave Sand another kick in the shins. "G'wan, scram," she urged.

"Nix," he replied out of the side of his mouth and through his false whiskers.

"Hit the road, ya big boof." She was about four feet high, frail and hollow-eyed. Around her neck hung a tray of cheap zombiemade cigarette lighters. "This is my corner!"

Sand lowered his battered guitar, then squatted to look her in the eye. "I have a particular reason for . . . ow!"

She'd booted him in the crotch. "Scat, get off my turf, you figgie."

"Whoa now." Sand caught hold of her thin arm. "We ought to be able to work out a financial agreement."

The disputed corner was directly across the street from a Colonel Fatso's Venusian Style Fried Wollo

47

Restaurant. In the bright front window a green chef
was grilling thick juicy wollo steaks while being
watched by a sidewalk audience of a half dozen tourists and Official Bums. This was in the heart of Safe
Zone 19, a sector rich with light signs, talk signs and
sublims.

Poker Annie's! flashed a high dangling light sign.

Flaming Youth.

Dirty Don's Den of Iniquity! Immediate Seating.

Trisex Hairstyling.

Dime Jig!

Torture Garden! Booths For Ladies!

Weber's Naked Ladies With Big Tits Club!

Floating and suspended blareboxes were crying out
messages into the gaudy night.

"Eat Till You Bust!"

"Get Your Ashes Hauled!"

"Go Off Your Diet!"

"Free Brainstim With Every Whipping!"

"Mock Suicides Hourly!"

"Lust!"

"Swill!"

"Read Books Dismissed As Trivial By Noted Critics!"

The golden-haired waif was scrutinizing Sand's
newbearded face. "That's a pisspoor set of whiskers
you got, mister."

"How'd you like to earn ten trubux?"

"You look sorta young to be a dirty old man."

"I'm fond of this corner," Sand explained. "I'll pay
you $10 for the use of it tonight."

The waif considered, tugging at her golden ringlets
with a grubby forefinger. "I don't know, jocko," she
said. "See, I'm sort of an institution hereabouts. Known
far and wide as Katie the Poor Little Butane Lighter
Girl. Suppose some tourists drop by on purpose to

take a gander and I ain't on my accustomed spot? 'Shinola! What's this gink in the spurious face fuzz doing on Katie's corner?' Bad for biz.''

"Twenty trubux."

"Sold."

From inside his raggedy tunic Sand drew out two tens. "Here, Katie." He handed her the cash, grinning thinly. "Now scoot."

"Hold your goonies," she advised, smoothing the two blue and yellow bills out on a clear spot on her tray. "We'll just make sure this ain't funny money." From underneath the tray Katie brought up a small coppery tube. She passed it, slowly and carefully, over each bill. "It'll bleep like johnnythunder if these are fakes."

Sand straightened up, readjusting the guitar he'd acquired at a pawnshop an hour ago. "They're genuine."

"Looks like they are, yeah. Thanks." She took a few steps away from him. "Listen, gunko, if anybody should ask for Sweetback Slim, he's working out of Deepsea Dawson's Pub tonight and Lectric Lana's sores ain't healed but they can have any of Slim's other clients. Got that? As for the numbers slips, I'll be at Busino's Brainstim Parlor for the rest of the evening."

"I'll pass that on to whomsoever asks," he promised.

"You ain't really down and out, are you?"

"Only for the moment."

"Let me give you one piece of advice. If you're too much of a wiseass, you don't last long around here." She hunched her thin shoulders and went walking away into the crowd.

Sand returned his attention to the cook in the fried wollo restaurant's window. This was a fellow named Freddie Sparr, a part-time freelance field agent for

Soldiers of Fortune, Inc. He was the gent most of the agents who'd come to grief on Fazenda had contacted. SOF maintained that Sparr checked out clean, but Sand wanted to watch him, talk to him later and make up his own mind.

". . . is it like a cow, daddy?"

"Sort of, only larger and furry."

"Like my own dear cow back home on Murdstone? Like Mrs. Moolywoopsie?"

"Well, only vaguely, Darin."

A portly greentoned tourist in a conventional three-piece cazsuit had halted on Sand's corner. His ten-year-old son was pudgy, too, clad in a two-piece space navysuit. The boy was watching Sparr grill steaks, a look of concern on his plump emerald face.

"I don't think I'd especially care to watch someone cooking up slices of Mrs. Moolywoopsie," said the lad. "Especially in a greasy window in the sleazy heart of the tenderloin."

"Wollos are different, Darin," he was assured by his father. "They're raised to be cooked. They no doubt look on it as their duty."

"Would you enjoy being fried in a public window?"

"Not especially, no."

"Then I don't imagine a wollo would either."

"Let's move on."

"This isn't much fun, daddy. I think momsy was right and we should've gone to Mars or Disneyplanet on our vacation instead of to this hellhole."

"You're close to coming of age, Kev, it's time you . . ."

They walked on.

"Sing something."

"Huh?"

A tipsy birdgirl in a sewdofur cloak was standing in front of Sand. She was alone, swaying slightly. "Sing me a sad song. I'll drop a coin into your cup. Isn't that how it works?"

"Usually," admitted Sand. "Thing is, I've just lost my voice and—"

"How come, how come, then, I can hear you? Riddle me this if you will."

"My singing voice is what I lost."

"Okay, play me a tune then. Something lowdown."

"Another of my sorrows, miss, is that my strumming and plucking hand is temporarily paralyzed."

"Geeze, you are sure in shitcan shape," the birdgirl observed, sharp peak ticking. "What you are in dire need of is job counseling. Here you are trying to earn a living as a sidewalk singer, but you can't sing nor can you—"

"I'll be better soon, meantime I don't want to lose my corner. So I'm—"

"I happen to be a job counselor," she told him, lurching unexpectedly to the left and then righting herself. "On my home planet of Peregrine, which is in the faroff Barnum System, I hold down the position of—"

"I appreciate your concern, miss, but I'm really not seeking much in the way of rehabilitation. Just drop a coin in the cup, if you will, and then—"

"You don't have to be rehabbed." She took hold of his tattered lapel with one unsteady claw. "You can remain a miserable bum, yet one who more fully utilizes his abilities. Now, can you maybe whistle?"

"Yes, but not in tune."

"Tap dance? Until your voice returns you ought to be able to earn a pretty penny by tapdancing here on—"

"Excuse me." He noticed that Freddie Sparr had left the display window of Colonel Fatso's and was exiting a sidedoor. "My shift just ended."

Sand shoved the helpful birdgirl gently aside and cut across the street. He began following the SOF contact through the glaring, noisy streets of the safe zone.

Somebody else was tailing Sparr.

A middle-sized humanoid, on the plump side, decked out in a two-piece suit of tatters. He walked with a lopsided shuffle, using a blackwood cane. He'd picked up the SOF field man when Sparr passed the alley mouth between Charlie Ting-a-Ling's Opium Den and an Eminent Victorians Pizza Theater.

Sand slowed, giving the tail more room to work between him and Sparr.

As he passed the pizza theater a half-sized mustached andy hailed him from the doorway. "Bully night, eh? Come on in and hear me deliver my big stick spiel," he invited.

"Not tonight, Teddy."

The plump man stooped to snatch up a kelpstogie butt. Anxious, no doubt, to add verisimilitude to his disguise.

As Sand followed in the wake of the two men he rubbed at his whiskered chin. "I know this second guy," he said to himself. "Yep, ran into him on Tarragon couple years back while I was working on that teleported diplomat job . . . his name's . . . Humberstone. Right, Lloyd Humberstone, used to work for Interplanet Pinkerton. But got fired for illegal brainscanning of witnesses . . . been scuffling, free-lancing ever since. You'd think the competition, whoever they may be, could do better than Lloyd Humberstone."

Up ahead Freddie Sparr was crossing a narrow stone-work bridge over a scummy canal.

Just short of the bridge was a dimlit place called the Whorehouse Warehouse. *Why Pay More?* inquired its dingy light sign. *No Frills Sex!* Next to this brix bordello was a thin dark lane.

Sand sprinted, caught up with the shuffling Humberstone exactly in front of the lane entrance. "Let's have a chat, Lloyd," he invited, getting an armlock on the freelance op and yanking him into the shadows.

"Easy, mate," muttered Humberstone. "I'm just a down and out bum, much like yourself. Ain't got no cash on me. Truth."

"Lloyd, you're much too softlooking to bring off the hobo dodge." Sand pushed him up against the brix wall.

"Ah, I got it now. You're one of them screwballs who murders innocent derelicts. Am I right?"

"Lloyd, I'm John Wesley Sand." He shed his guitar, took hold of the man's shoulders.

"Johnny," said Humberstone. "What an unusual co-incidence this is, old man. Two crack freelances encountering each other on this godforsaken planet. Wellsir . . . we'll have to have lunch one of these days. I'm staying at the Statler-Flophouse over on Dream Street. Right now, though, Johnny, I'm a bit late for a business engage—"

"Why you following Sparr?"

"Who?" His eyes went wide. "Don't quite get your drift, old fellow. I'm not tagging a soul, human or otherwise. If I don't toddle off now, though, I'm going to—"

"I'm a mite pressed for time myself." Sand fished a truth disc out of his pocket.

"What are you contemplating, old boy?" Humberstone

caught a flash of the disc as Sand moved to slap it against his temple. He tried to swat it away.

Too late. The disc took him over and he had to tell Sand what he knew and what he was up to.

Chapter 8

"There, now the air is not quite as noxious as previously," observed Munson. He poked yet another button on the control dash of their rented landvan. "But this cabin still reeks of decaying marine life. Perhaps the supplemental aircirc system will filter out the rest of the noxious odors from without."

"Think maybe what we're also getting is the remains of the lunch of the last bunch who rented this clunk." Sand was hunched in the passenger seat, knees up, and going over the latest report from Hack O'Hara.

"Ah, then in that case...." The android's gloved fingertips went skittering along the control panel. "We shall call upon the super freshener toggles. Lillacs ... sandalwood ... and ... um ... fresh-baked bread. How is that, sir?"

Sand sneezed. "Blends well with the fish odor."

They were rolling rapidly across a fog-ridden stretch

of desolate land. It was mostly bleak fields and blighted woods all about. Swirls of greenish smoke drifted up from one weedy field, a yellowish mist hung over another. Stunted scavenger birds were perched on the leafless branches of the gray trees.

"You were not, if I may point out the fact, in a very communicative mood when you returned last evening," said Munson, guiding the van around a swampy patch in the rundown road. "Beyond advising me that we were to embark this morning for the farmland area, you spoke little. Were your peregrinations among the lowlife fruitful?"

"Turn off those damn freshener nozzles," requested Sand.

"We happen to be journeying through one of the largest garbage dumping areas on the planet, nay, on several planets," reminded the android servant. "One would think a few pleasant aromas might gladden rather than—"

"I'm getting fresh pumpernickel mist down my neck."

"Very well." Munson, sighing, shut off the nozzles. "You were on the brink of enlightening me as to what you learned last evening."

Sand glanced out at a dumping ground littered with the remains of old skycars and servos. A tiny man with an extra arm was scurrying up a pile of twisted, rusting cookbots. "Gent named Lloyd Humberstone was hired three days ago by the PEO," he said finally. "They wanted the local Soldiers of Fortune contact watched and reported on."

"Only three days ago?"

"Before that a regular Political Espionage part-timer was on the job."

"May one hazard the guess that he was sent on to glory?"

"Seems likely, since he's vanished," replied Sand. "PEO was desperate, so they hired a crumbum like Humberstone until they can hop another of their men out here to Fazenda."

"Why, did you persuade Humberstone to divulge, is the PEO killing off SOF agents?"

"They aren't. A third party is in on this."

"And what of the listening device planted in our cabin on the spacejumper. Was that the work of this third party?"

"Nope, PEO did that," said Sand with a frown, "and I don't know why I never spotted anybody on that damn ship who was in cahoots with them. Probably one of the humanoid stewards or—"

"Ah, the folly of human cupidity," said Munson, whose attention was on the ruined housing development they were driving by.

Partly hidden by high orange and green weeds and a thick bluish mist, the twenty or so small faded cottages were fronted by a long-defunct light sign that read *Dump Village, Economy Housing For All!*

"This goes back fifteen years or so," said Sand. "When the government hereabouts was attempting to persuade the poor to relocate on these stretches of land between dump sites."

"Ah, there appears to be an even viler one coming up on our left. 'Toxic Acres Estates. Live Cheaply Albeit Dangerously!' "

Sand returned to going over, and decoding in his head, the report from Hack. "The relocation scheme didn't work very well."

"So one surmises. Ah, there lies a posher tract on yonder hill. Garbage Heights, eh? And nearby a brazen billboard that inquires, 'What's So Bad About Mutating?' "

"Oy," remarked Sand.

"Beg pardon, sir?"

"According to Hack, Political Espionage is going to send an agent named Typhoon Tyson out here to track the Brandywine daughter."

"Is he likely to be as offensive as his name?"

Sand nodded. "Big hulking guy, dedicated to his job. He's so damn aggressive he makes Glory Forbes look demure."

"Speaking of the young lady, sir," said the android, "one can not help remarking that perhaps you, under the spell of her rather obvious physical attractions, tended to overestimate her capabilities as an investigative reporter. We have quite successfully eluded the young woman ever since we first—"

"Never underestimate Glory," advised Sand.

"I am, as you know if you perused my accompanying manual and instruction sheets with the attention they deserve, not at all vain," said Munson. "Yet I can not help crowing a bit at how we have managed to keep her from—"

"Slow down. Frumas on the road up ahead."

"Ah, so there is." Munson lifted his foot from the accelerator. "The trouble appears to be centered on that disreputable wayside cafe up there. The Flying Slepyan Brothers' Truckers & Slavers Roadside Restaurant. Not an especially catchy name for an eating place, one feels. I am at a loss as to why the word flying was inserted into—"

"The brothers, most of them, used to be with a circus."

The cafe was a large dome-shaped affair, squatting at the side of the roadway and surrounded by gnarled trees and thriving multicolor weeds. In the mucky parking lot at least ten stiff-walking men were marching in a slow circle waving signs. Three burly waiters, plus a catman chef, were trying to force them away. Some of the activity had spilled over onto the road.

" 'Unfair To Zombies!' proclaim most of their signs," said Munson, slowing further to avoid the zombies who were being edged onto the road. "Is one to infer that this is a labor dispute?"

"Just drive on by, no matter what sort of dispute it is."

All at once two of the zombies lurched, then came running right into the path of the landvan.

"My aunt!" Munson clutched the drivestik, swerved the van.

The vehicle bounced, shuddered, went rocketing clean off the roadway. It didn't stop until it smacked hard into the broad trunk of a sturdy blueoak.

"One must apologize for this slipshod example of driving, sir," said the android as the landvan ceased rattling. "I am not used, I fear, to reanimated corpses bounding unexpectedly into—"

Zzzzzzizzzzzzz!

The entire window on Munson's side of the cab melted clean away. Then a pale hand came thrusting in, clutching a compact disabler gun.

Before Sand could even dive across the seat and make a grab for the gun, its yellowish beam had hit the android full in the head.

Munson said, "I say, this is . . ." and then gave off an ominous grinding-to-a-halt noise, slumping back in his seat.

"Compliments of Miss Glory Forbes," grinned the zombie at the window.

Chapter
9

Arms folded, Sand leaned against the van and watched the zombies go shuffling away along the road. Their feet produced small slurping sounds on the mucky ground.

Sand had moved the landvan over to the Flying Slepyans parking lot, after stretching the disabled Munson out on a backseat.

"Looks like Glory Forbes has managed to toss a spanner in the works," he acknowledged to himself, glancing up at a brilliant crimson carrion crow who was eyeing him from the domed roof of the wayside cafe. "I'm going to have to live by my wits for a spell, which she seems to think'll give her an advantage."

All the sophisticated weapons and surveillance gear built into the android were useless for now.

"How's a cup of nearcaf sound?" called the small, dark man who poked his head out the kitchen door.

"As opposed to what, Nels?"

The man stepped out into the hazy day, cup of steaming beverage in his left hand, and squinted at Sand. "Holy gee, if it isn't John Wesley Sand."

"It is." He crossed the lot toward Nels Slepyan. "How much did you have to do with this ambush?"

Nels said, "Is that what it was? That's sure a relief, meaning no offense. We've been trying to figure out why the zombie culinary workers local pulled this demonstration, since we just gave their kickback chairman a hefty . . . but enough of our mundane troubles, John. What brings you to Fazenda?"

"You know a lady named Molly Yronsyde?"

Nels looked to the left, to the right, then into the cup. "Believe I'll drink this myself," he said, taking a long sip. "Last time I saw you was on Tarragon, when we were traveling with the Shestack Sisters Circus. You were out there working on a missing relics caper for Pope Sally XII of Barnum and—"

"I'm not in the mood for biography," cut in Sand. "I've got a damaged android and—"

"*That's* no problem. Gonzaga'll take care of that in a jiffy."

"Who's Gonzaga?"

"E. Power Gonzaga."

"So?"

"Runs a hardware store up the road a piece. He can—"

"Nels, this is a very high-class android. I don't want the local handyman tinkering with—"

"Listen, John, this is *the* E. Power Gonzaga," explained Nels. "He used to be in charge of the Hellquad government's robotics program until he became disenchanted and retired out here to the dumps to contemplate on the infinite folly and idiocy of humanity, as he puts it."

"He can get my mechanical man working again?"

"In a jiffy, as I may have mentioned earlier. We met him through the peace movement."

"What peace movement?"

Nels drank some more of the nearcaf. "After my brothers, Nate, Ned, Nayland and Nugent, all became too obese for the trapeze act . . . it's my fault in a way, since it's my irresistible homestyle cooking that contributed to—"

"Where's Gonzaga come in?"

"After our act was grounded, I went out on my own for a spell. As Nerveless Nels the Human Canonball. That was on Fumaza, an even worse hole than this planet. There's a very active antiweaponry movement out there and they didn't even like me. They took to picketing my act and one of the pickets was Gonzaga. You know how it goes, you trade a few punches with a guy and you get to be chums and—"

"Nope, that's never happened to me. How far is this store?"

"Nine, ten miles up the road there."

"Okay, I'll dump Munson on him."

"That the name of your andy? Sounds somewhat dull and prosaic. Me, I favor socko names like Ajax, Maximo, Rex or—"

"Now tell me about Molly Yronsyde." Sand put his hand on the smaller man's shoulder.

"Here's some sound advice for—"

Kathump!

A resounding thud came from within the restaurant.

Nels shook his head. "That'd be Nayland," he said ruefully. "He just won't admit he's too hefty for trapeze work. Every now and then, when the mood hits him, he rigs one up with the same unfortunate results. I've often—"

"I want to have a talk with Molly Yronsyde," Sand told him. "Thing is, several gents who've attempted that of late have ceased to exist. I was planning on having my android kidnap her or—"

"She's a very tough person," warned Nels in a lowered voice. "You don't want to mess with a lady who carries a bullwhip with her at all times. Not to mention an impressive array, so I hear, of concealed weapons."

"Her ranch is about thirty miles north of here."

"Sure, in one of the Ranchland Sectors. No garbage allowed in those parts," said Nels. "She's not there, though, so you may as well just hop in your van and go back to—"

"Where is she?"

Nels finished off the nearcaf, wiped his lips on his sleeve. "We've been close and intimate friends for many a year, John, so—"

"Nope, we're just acquaintances, Nels. Meaning I might do you physical harm if you don't fill me in on—"

"She's at the Salvage Island Country Club by now."

"Where's that?"

Pulling free of Sand, Nels pointed in the direction of the misty woodlands beyond the parking lot. "That way, some twenty miles or thereabouts. One of those projects intended to beautify the dumps. Fancy island built in the middle of a toxic waste burying ground. Didn't work out too well. First batch of guests who stayed there started glowing in the dark the second night they—"

"Why's Molly there?"

"A meeting, a secret meeting. After all these years the place isn't as dreadful as it once was, folks use it for sneaky meetings now and then," said Nels. "This particular get-together, if you must know, John, involves several of the big ranchers and some of the top rustlers. Has something to do with the ranchers buying their stolen grouts, cows, wollos and such back."

"How come you know about it?"

"Well . . ."

"Nels?"

Kathump!

"You have to admire Nayland's determination."

"You were saying?"

"As a matter of fact, we're catering the meeting. I have to make a hundred GLT . . . that's grout, lettuce and tomato . . . sandwiches, two hundred wolloburgers and sundry other delicacies and get the whole shebang over there before sundown." He started to turn away. "Thus, I don't have any more time to gab. Sorry about your being waylaid so close to our establishment."

"Nels, you've got a new assistant. A personable young man who's going to help you deliver the food."

Nels frowned up at him. "You?"

"Yep."

"Well, then you may as well lend a hand with the sandwiches," he said. "And if Molly Yronsyde kills you graveyard dead, don't blame me."

Chapter
10

A bluish lizard man, wearing bib overalls and a venerable straw hat, was rocking slowly in a creaky wicker rocker on the porch of Gonzaga's Hardware & Notions Store. He was whittling intently as he rocked, carving some sort of small figure out of a chunk of yellow wood.

"Gonzaga inside?" inquired Sand as he started up the swayback realwood steps.

"Far as I know, stranger. Leastwise . . . yow!" He'd cut his scaly left hand. "Dang, that there's the trouble with mewts."

"You're a mutant?"

"Naw, don't be a blamed idiot," said the lizard man. "I just carve the dang critters, out of dumler wood." He held up his work in progress. "This here's going to be a three-armed dump scavenger. Carving that there third arm just right is a bugger. One slip of the old knife and you nick your finger. I'm Moot."

"Beg pardon?"

"Name is Moot," amplified the whittler. "Figures I turn out is knowed as Moot's Mewts. Sell right well specially to tourists. Moot's Mewts."

"Pleased to meet you, Moot." Sand went on into the store.

It was dim and shadowy, crowded with shelves and display cases that held a jumble of nuts, bolts, nails, tools. Pots and pans dangled from the low ceiling in considerable profusion.

"Hey, you groutjawed beanpole, did you wipe your clodhopper feet?" called a thin, raspy voice from behind the counter.

"Guess I didn't."

"Supposed to use the mat on the porch, nitwit. Says Welcome! Have A Happy Day! on it. Any halfwit ought to be able to figure out the purpose—"

"You Gonzaga?"

"Who the devil else'd I be, standing behind the counter in Gonzaga's Hardware & Notions Store, wearing a smock that has EPG emblazoned on the pencil and pen pocket?"

"Thought you might be one of Moot's Mewts."

"Smartass," remarked Gonzaga, who was a small leathery man with considerable white frizzly hair atop his large head. "Offplanet wiseguy is how I size you up."

"Exactly," admitted Sand. "Nels Slepyan tells me you—"

"How is that walleyed former projectile?"

"As well as can be expected."

"Lousy act he had, worst human cannonball I ever saw. Even his trajectory was—"

"You fix androids."

"Don't take a wizard to figure that out." He jerked a

stained thumb at the hand-lettered sign on the wall behind him. Expert Android Repairs. Quick Dependable Service!

Sand halted a few feet from the counter. "Letter that yourself?"

"You got some snide criticism to make of it, outlander?"

"You got your upper and lower case letters all mixed up."

"I'm an artist, not a typesetter," replied Gonzaga. "Where's your android?"

"Out in the van."

"What's the problem?"

"Somebody used a disabler on him."

When Gonzaga nodded his frazzled hair flickered. "You look like the kind of ninny who'd provoke that sort of thing. Who are you anyway?"

"John Wesley Sand."

Gonzaga's frazzled eyebrows climbed. "The notorious mercenary." He picked up a swatter, took a swing at a small green insect that was scurrying up a jar of jawbreakers, missed. "I've heard of you, Sand."

"Shall I bring him in?"

Unexpectedly, Gonzaga leaped from behind the counter. "I'll come out and take a gander before we move him," he said. "What disreputable and dishonorable assignment brings you to Fazenda?"

"A confidential one."

"Even you freelance agents get to acting mysterious and sly." He went stomping across the plank floor, headed outside. "You better sweep up those halfwit shavings, Moot."

"Always do, Gonz. You know ... Yow! Dang if I didn't slice myself again."

Uninvited, Gonzaga yanked the rear doors of the

landvan open. "Aha, a Munson, eh? You must be charging your poor client a pretty penny." Grunting, he climbed inside and stood beside the stretched out android.

"You'll find this one has a few added features that aren't usual with—"

"Let me examine the darn patient and don't heckle me," suggested Gonzaga as he began to prod and poke Munson.

". . . message . . . came in . . ." muttered the felled android. ". . . from . . . Hack . . . Hack . . ."

"Strange cough he's got." Gonzaga continued to poke.

"Wait a minute." Sand eased up next to the android. "Munson, have you got something new from Hack?"

". . . can't print it out . . . think Hack's gone . . . since I long since cracked your infantile code . . . gone bonkers . . ."

"What did he send?"

"Warning you about the little man in the jar . . . does not, if you don't mind my saying, make any . . ." Munson ceased to talk, began making a low buzzing sound through his plaz nose.

Straightening up, Gonzaga watched Sand for a few seconds. "I can fix him. Take a day, perhaps two," he said finally. "Do you know what he was alluding to?"

"Afraid I do, yep."

"If you're involved in some kind of espionage work, Sand, then you better go very carefully," advised Gonzaga. "The little man in the jar is a nasty scoundrel known as Micro. I encountered him once during my days with the Hellquad government. He is, without doubt, one of the most ruthless freelance agents in the universe."

"So I've heard," said Sand, wishing Munson had been able to provide a few more details.

• • •

The crimson crow had been joined by two colleagues and all three were pecking at something small at the edge of the Slepyan parking lot.

When Sand climbed out of the landvan, the crows went scattering up and away into the hazy afternoon.

There were no other vehicles parked on the lot and, Sand noticed as he approached the entrance, the plaz walls of the cafe had been blacked.

Stuck on the inside of the door was a hastily lettered sign. *Closed Due To Sudden Illness In Family.*

Sand crouched, picked the lock on the door and slipped inside the cafe. He went to the storeroom, the wooden floor of which had a large jagged hole in it, and selected two fat sewdohams from the several that hung on wallhooks. Tucking one under each arm, he went outside again.

Sand, grinning, returned to the van and got in the driveseat. He tossed the hams on the passenger seat, then flipped a toggle on the dash that activated a small scanner screen. A tiny blinking light appeared, moving slowly. It was the signal being given off by the tracking bug Sand had planted in Nels' delivery landtruck before heading for Gonzaga's hardware store.

He started his engine, drove the landvan onto the narrow road that went winding through the misty woodlands.

Chapter
11

He lost the sunlight completely. A few minutes into the woods and a thick grayish mist closed in on Sand and his bouncing, jolting landvan.

The branches of the trees twisted and interlocked over the thin roadway, some sort of faintly glowing moss festooned a great many of them. Several forlorn and featherless birds were roosting on the zigzag branches of a tree that was almost completely covered with white, dimly luminous moss. In the patches of shadow between the tree trunks small cliques of fat white rats lurked and watched Sand's progress. There was a strong stench, foul and sweet, that hung over the woodlands and insinuated itself into the cab through his missing window.

"Easy to see why too many tourists don't get out this way," Sand said to himself as he drove toward the country club, following Nels Slepyan's electronic trail.

He was a bit unsettled at the possibility that the

agent known as Micro might be hunting for Julia Brandywine. Although Sand had never tangled with Micro, he'd heard a hell of a lot about him. As a result of a freak accident in a microminiaturizing factory on Murdstone some nine years ago, Micro had been shrunk down to the size of a speck. He'd vowed not to let his handicap hurt his career in freelance espionage and intelligence work and he'd succeeded. But, embittered by his accident, Micro became absolutely ruthless. He traveled around in a small metal jug that provided protection and life support, amplified his now tiny voice and projected, when need be, his image on any handy plain surface. The last time Sand had heard, Micro and his jug were looked after by an especially nasty onetime Zero-G wrestler named Strangler Selznick. It seemed more than likely that Micro was responsible for the deaths of Sand's predecessors.

"Wonder whom he's working for."

The mist and the stench grew stronger as Sand drove deeper into the woods. The rats got bolder, some of them charging out from among the trees and attempting to bite the landvan.

Roughly an hour after entering the woodlands Sand crested a rise and saw an artificial lake stretching away below. Out in the exact middle sat a small island with a huge, sprawling towered and turreted brix building at its exact center.

An arching neowood bridge led from the near shore to the island, crossing over the green, scummy waters of the lake. Leaning against the gate of the bridge were two husky lizard men in groutboy outfits, gunbelts, high-crowned hats and chaps. They were watching Sand's approach, not cordially.

"Hold 'er right there, dude," warned one when Sand and the van were a dozen yards from the bridge. He drew twin silver kilguns, spun them on green fingers and pointed them at Sand.

Sand hit the brake, killed the engine. "Boy, am I glad I found this place," he said out his glazless window, grinning. Despite what Glory Forbes had said, he felt he could still affect a guileless look. "I been worried near sick."

Both the big lizard men came bowlegging over to him, spurs jingling.

"Keep your dang mitts where we can see 'em, mister," instructed the one who was apparently the spokesman for the duo. "Otherwise I'll be obliged to use these here shooting irons on your carcass."

"Can't keep my hands in sight if I'm going to unload these darn hams."

"What the dickens you jawing about, waddie?"

"Listen, did my boss come through here?"

"Who might he be?"

"Nels Slepyan. Middle-sized dark-complected gent accompanied by several hundred sandwiches."

"You must mean that caterer feller. Sure, he arrived more than an hour back."

Ignoring the guns, Sand gathered up one of the sewdohams and hopped down off of the cab. "See, Mr. Slepyan was so anxious to rush your food out here that he forgot the hams." He held this one up to them.

The lizard man's snout wrinkled. "I'm a veggie myself, pardner."

"Now there's a coincidence for you, so am I," confided Sand. "Unfortunately, some of the folks at this shindig aren't. When Mr. Slepyan gets ready to prepare a plate of sliced sewdoham for the festive board, he's going to be ticked off at not finding any ham. Who you think he's going to blame?"

"He'll more than likely say it's your fault, sure,"

said the lizard man, nodding. "That's the way of the dang world."

"Surely is."

"Okay, waddie," he gestured at the van and then the bridge with his left-hand gun. "Get in that buggy of yours and cross on over. Kitchen's round the back of that pile of brix. Tell Lucas, he's on guard there, that the Dumpsite Kid said you was okay."

"That's a right catchy name, Dumpsite." Grinning at him and his partner, Sand carried the ham back into the van.

"What's this going to do to my reputation?" inquired Nels, who was watching Sand stir a knockout powder into Molly Yronsyde's mug of greenbeer.

"Better to occupy your mind," advised Sand, "with thoughts of what I'm going to do to your corporeal self if you don't start cooperating."

"I've had, really, a lot of things on my mind, John. The main reason I didn't bring you was that I forgot." He started again to arrange the purple garnish on the platters of sandwiches sitting on the long white kitchen table. "Catering this affair, helping get Nayland out of the cellar . . . Did I mention he dropped clean through to the cellar the last time he fell off his makeshift trapeze—"

"Get into the buffet room now," Sand said, returning the drink to the copper tray, which held several schooners, flagons and tumblers filled with liquors. "Fill this drink order, make dead sure Molly gets this beer."

"John, if people start thinking my food causes you to fall over dead after—"

"She won't fall dead, trust me, but merely pass out."

"Well, that's bad enough. There aren't all that many lucrative catering jobs in this godforsaken—"

"Do it," urged Sand. "Soon as she falls over, I'll enter and explain that I'm a physician and haul her—"

"You don't have a medical aura. There are a lot of mean and nasty people out there, well over a hundred of them. I doubt you're going to fool all those mean and nasty ranchers, mean and nasty rustlers, mean and nasty attorneys and—"

"Serve the drinks, Nels."

"I should have stuck with cannonball work." He lifted up the drink tray, took a slow deep breath and went pushing through the swing door.

When Sand deposited the hefty Molly on the glaz sofa in the untenanted suite, her bullwhip fell free from its resting place in her broad belt.

He kicked it aside and crouched beside the stocky lady rancher. From his pocket he extracted a truth disc and attached it to her temple.

After waiting a moment, he asked, "Molly, what happened to Jill Gaynes?"

Molly's voice was husky and blurred. "The poor little tyke," she sighed, eyes tight shut. "I loved her dearly."

"Where is she?"

"Dead and gone," was the answer. "Yes, we buried her frail body in the north forty beneath a simple headstone. The sorrow has been hard to live with. That was four years ago."

Narrowing one eye, Sand asked her, "What'd the inscription on the tombstone say?"

Molly's head rolled from side to side twice. "Come again?"

"The inscription, what did you have engraved?"

"I don't remember."

"Has a fellow named Micro been calling on you?"

"No."

Sand tugged off the woman's ornate boots, then her woolly socks. Between the big toe and next one on her left foot he located a tiny puckered blue dot. "Yep, looks like Micro gave her a shot and then planted a fake memory," he said.

Frisking himself, Sand located a small metal case. He took a miniature hypogun out of it.

Molly twitched on the sofa when the shot went in between her toes.

Sand put the hypogun away, stood, paced the big room. From the view window he could see the lake, the bridge and the Dumpsite Kid. A bloated dead fish was floating near the far shore.

Back beside Molly he said, "Okay, the stuff ought to be working by now. When was Micro here?"

"That lowdown galoot," she said in a droning voice. "Him and that there Strangler toady of his. Claimed they had a lucrative shady cattle deal for me, but all they had up their sleeves was shooting me full of foul drugs and poking around in my private thoughts and memories."

"When?"

"More than a week ago."

"Know where Micro is now?"

"Hunting for that brat."

"Did you tell them where she is?"

"Hellsfire, I got no idea where she is and don't give a damn," said Molly, a touch of anger showing in her droning, drugged voice. "I should never of agreed to take her in at all. Meanspirited and ornery she was, independent and wouldn't take orders. Never did her share of the chores around the damn ranch, never come near to earning her keep. Always reading or pretending to be writing books when she wasn't vamping the hands and flirting something awful. Nope nosir, I don't miss that little bitch one bit."

"Where'd she go?"

"I sold her."

He squatted down nearer to her. "To whom?"

"Only got a lousy 1000 trubux, but I'd of almost paid them to take her off my hands."

"Who?"

"Moms Goodtime, Inc. That chain of bordellos," she answered. "They got seventy-two thriving outlets on the four Hellquad planets. They could have come up with more than a thousand."

"When was this?"

"Four years ago."

Sand said, "Know if she's still working at one of those places?"

"She sure as hell ain't. Nosir, wasn't on the dang job more than a few months when she up and sweet talked a cyborg pimp into running off with her."

"Any notion where she went?"

"Several."

"How's that?"

"After she'd been gone near a year my kin on Murdstone asked after her. They was sort of anxious for some reason to contact her again," she said. "Course I couldn't up and tell 'em I'd sold her to a bagnio, so I just made out like she'd run off. Wellsir, they was willing to fork over $1500 to have her hunted for."

"You did that?"

"Started it off, but we used up the whole damn $1500, plus another almost $400 of my own I never could get back out of them tightwads, before we found out much of anything. Her we never located."

"What did you learn, Molly?"

"Them Moms Goodtime joints don't keep too good records. See, at about the same time that Jill hightailed it, couple other young ladies of her general description also slipped away from one of the houses or another. By the time I got my gumshoes on the case we couldn't be sure which of them flitting girls was Jill. One of 'em went off to Farpa and was last heard of working as a wrestler, another had a job for a while on Farridor doing some sort of dippy social work, the third was maybe working with a circus on Fumaza. Would've cost us a stewpot of money to follow up all them leads all over the Hellquad. Turned out my kin wasn't *that* eager, so I let the whole thing drop. Good riddance, I says."

"You told all that to Micro?"

"Didn't have no choice. That little runt pumped me full of truth drugs, same as you're doing."

"He must've had somebody here on Fazenda to knock off the SOF agents as they arrived," reflected Sand. "Meanwhile he took off on the girl's trail, and the bastard has a headstart of several days."

The door of the suite suddenly swung open. "How's the little lady doing?" inquired an obese catman in a groutskin fringesuit.

"Just fine," said Sand. "If you'll sit with her for a spell, I'll go fetch some additional medication from my van."

Chapter
12

The night mist came rolling along the roadway at
him. It was thick, glowed faintly green and smelled of
rot and dead soil. The beams of his van lights briefly
illuminated animals, and occasional people, who were
lurking at the sides of the twisting road. Stunted blond
raccoons watched him pass, a candy-striped possum
stood up on its hind feet and seemed to be pleading.
Farther along three gaunt welfs in tattered worksuits
sat around a peat fire grilling a cat. One of them made
a keening noise as the landvan came speeding by, left
the fireside and tried running after Sand.

". . . handout . . . handout . . ."

Sand kept moving.

If you let yourself feel anything, any sympathy, you'd
forever be getting sidetracked.

When he reached Gonzaga's hardware store and
parked, a one-armed man who glowed pale silver came
stumbling out of the shadowy brush.

". . . help me out, mister . . ." he begged. His face was splotched with cuts and sores, his clothes smeared with muck and blood. ". . . just enough to buy oblivion for . . ."

Sand went up the steps two at a time, pushed into the store.

"Okay, okay," called the glowing man from outside, "screw you then, you heartless son of a bitch!"

Moot was tending the counter, concentrating on applying a plyodaid to a new cut on his right hand. "Danged if I ain't been a bundle of nerves all day," he said. "Been cutting myself up one side and down the other."

"Art can do that to you sometimes. Where's Gonzaga?"

The big green whittler pointed a bandaged thumb toward an open lighted doorway to his left. "Back in the workshop, tinkering away with that there snooty andy of yours."

"Much obliged."

"Sometimes," observed Moot, "I get to wishing to heck I wasn't making my living carving mewts. Looking at them all the time is starting to give me the heebie jeebies for fair."

Munson, wearing nothing at all, was stretched out on a floating white plaz table in the middle of the low narrow workroom. The rest of the place was a jumble of electronics gear, tool cabinets and cartons of cooking ware. There were computer terminals, control panels and a few things Sand couldn't exactly identify.

"Not very blinking efficient," remarked Gonzaga without looking up from his work. He had the android's chest wide open. "Good deal of useless duplication in here, Sand. I will refrain on commenting on the dippiness of giving a mechanical man a full set of sex organs."

"Are you progressing?"

"Naturally," he replied. "They used a cheap disabler on him. I'll have him working by this time tomorrow."

"Can't wait." Sand leaned his backside against the work table.

"Don't jiggle, dimbulb. And if you know of a better man for the job on this dimwitted planet, go to him."

"It's not that," explained Sand. "But I have to take off right away, maybe have three planets to hit."

"Micro involved in this?"

"Yep, and he's several jumps ahead of me."

"Retire," advised Gonzaga. "Open a hardware store in some remote and blighted sector, forget your troubles, let the world pass you by."

"Can't do that," said Sand. "Don't have the aptitude for it anyway."

"Chances are damn good Micro'll finish you off."

"I doubt a guy who travels in a jug can beat me." Sand began to prowl the room. "Reason I need Munson now is I want to use some of his built-in equipment to communicate with the other Hellquad planets."

"He won't be ready for that until late tomorrow."

"I've got a few contacts on the other garden spots in this system. I want them to check on the progress of Micro."

Gonzaga came up from his work, frazzled hair flickering. "Hell, use my telekom for that."

"I don't want the local government to know what I'm up to. They monitor all—"

"Do I look to be as big a mooncalf as you?" he asked. "When I design my own personal telekom, you can be damn sure nobody can eavesdrop. Go sit in that sprung sofa chair yonder, turn on the switch that has the twist of red ribbon around it. I assume you know how to take it from there."

"Sure, thanks."

"And I'll only charge you my offpeak rates."

"Noble of you." Sand climbed into the chair, faced the knee-high and fairly unorthodox communications console.

"I've been contemplating the situation all day," said Gonzaga, "and concluded that, as dim and inept as you are, I'd rather be on your side than Micro's."

Chapter
13

The ratman touched the bill of his gold-braided cap, bowing deferentially. "Compliments of Madam Captain, Mr. Sand, and will you join her at her table for dinner?"

Sand had just crossed the threshold of the spacecargo ship's low-ceilinged dining room. "Be delighted," he told the first mate.

"Right this way, sir." First Mate Sopkin led him through the small maze of close-packed tables. "Be a good notion, by the way, if you keep the quips about transsexuals down to a bare minimum during chow. Also hold off on all but the most good-natured badinage pertaining to wild-eyed and completely goofy religious hucksters, muckraking and unscrupulous journalism and the degrading and ruining of the helpless working classes by blackhearted plutocrats. Enjoy your meal, sir."

Sand settled into the only empty chair at the small round table and the first mate, with another polite bow, went scurrying away. "Good evening all," Sand began, "I'm John Wes . . . Damn!"

Sitting across from him, and smiling guilelessly, was Glory Forbes.

"How's that again, lubber?" inquired the captain, who seemed to be a husky woman of middle years. She wore a two-piece blue navysuit.

"This is John Wesley Sand," supplied Glory. "Well-known man about space."

"Zappo!" exclaimed the slender blue-haired girl next to Sand. "just like in all the romantic spaceyarns I've read and thrilled to. Lovers reunited on romantic old spacecargo bucket. This is really double rosco!"

"Is that what's going on, mate?" inquired the captain as she tapped ashes off her fat orange cigar. "You two lubbers are using my *Space Queen* to shack up on? Because I don't tolerate any fancy—"

"We're just friends," Sand assured her. "Our relationship is spiritual rather than physical."

"Oh, double barf," remarked the bluehead. "This is very wunky, since I was expecting a large scale romance to—"

"Allow me to commend you, brother," said the remaining guest at the table. He was a large man, sporting a full red beard and wearing a three-piece green clericsuit. "I am none other than the Most Sanctified Reverend Mailorder McManus. You've no doubt witnessed and been moved by my Sacred Hour of Donations television show, which airs on some 426 stations throughout the universe."

"I haven't, no," admitted Sand. "Really don't watch too much—"

"Mr. Sand's a man of action," explained Glory just as her soup was delivered by a toadman steward.

"Zappo!" The bluehead bounced in her chair. "This

is a romance afterall. I can tell that from the snide way you use when talking about him, Miss Forbes. That masks, as it always does in romances, a deeprooted yearning for—"

"Actually, no, Barni," said Glory firmly.

"Don't be an ooze," said Barni Sutt. "I've read tons of romances and I know that nasty hateful remarks directed at one person by another person of the opposite sex . . . Oh, double barf. I wasn't supposed to mention opposite sexes. Sorry, Captain Annie."

"Stow it, kid," said Space Tug Annie. "I'm not self-conscious anymore. At first, when I woke up and realized I now had seventy-two pairs of men's shoes that were no longer useful, not to mention paid-up memberships in several men's clubs and all, I was a bit taken aback. I'm more resigned now. Plus which the bastards settled for a tidy sum out of court."

Mailorder McManus, who sat on the other side of Sand, explained in a low voice, "Our unfortunate captain used to be a man until an unforeseen side effect of a new birth control potion transformed him into the attractive, if hefty, lady you see before you."

"The only drawback," said Annie, puffing on her cigar, "is trying to get a command. There's a real prejudice against sexchangers in the space navy. That explains why I'm still on this tug, making cargo and passenger hauls to a stinkhole like Fumaza."

"I have enjoyed several trips on your *Space Queen*," said McManus, "bringing my teams of missionaries out to Fumaza from Fazenda. And I have always found your ship to be . . . shipshape, Captain Annie." He gestured toward a nearby table with his beringed right hand.

Sitting there were four men in green suits and with long red beards.

"Is that a coincidence" asked Sand, starting in on his wollo and nearrice soup. "That all your missionaries have red whiskers?"

The reverend rocked back in his chair, gave a smiling shake of his head. "I see you really aren't familiar with the marvelous work I am doing," he said. "I am, Mr. Sand, the head of the Redbearded Hooghly Sect, and it is my divine mission to spread the pious teachings of the most Sacred Hooghly throughout the universe, from sinful planet to sinful planet."

"Hooghly had a red beard, did he?"

"Ah, this is very salutory, to realize there are many denizens of the universe who are woefully ignorant of Hooghly and his great thoughts," said Reverend McManus. "No, sir, Hooghly was a parrot."

"A parrot." Sand nodded and turned his attention to his soup.

"Mr. Sand is probably wondering how the red beards come in," suggested Glory helpfully.

"Hooghly once said," explained McManus, "in his famous *Sermon From The Birdcage #26*, 'Awk,awk! There's something about a bloke with a red beard that perks me up.' "

"If you ask me," put in Barni, "it's very wunky to let a bird tell you how to—"

"Ah, but Hooghly was not an ordinary parrot," said McManus patiently. "Here, let me give you a copy of one of our inspirational publications. Ordinarily this would cost you a Love Donation of twenty-six trudollars, but for a limited time only . . . um . . . forgive me. No, my dear, I am giving this marvelous book to you for absolutely nothing." From inside his green jacket he took a fat paper-covered book.

Gingerly, after setting aside her soup spoon, Barni accepted it. "*Hooghly Wants a Cracker & 99 Other*

Divinely Inspired Sayings of the Most Blessed Parrot Sage. That's a double barf of a title. Can you fancy anybody asking their home bookprinter for that?"

"What say we stow the religious gab," said the captain. "Sand, what brings you to take the trip to a craphat planet like Fumaza."

Sand was watching Glory. "It's nothing more than a pleasure jaunt," he answered.

The spacetramp's saloon was even smaller than the dining room. A single view window looked out onto the black infinity of space and the rest of the plaz walls were covered with faded travel posters inviting visits to planets in systems far from the Hellquad. The bartender was a four-armed green Martian.

Three of the four redbearded missionaries sat together at a lopsided table drinking mineral water and quoting Hooghly.

Sand was at a corner table by himself.

"Zappo!" exclaimed Barni Sutt when she noticed him. She came hurrying over with her foam-topped tumbler of greenale. "I was hoping I'd find you here, Sandy."

"Sand," he corrected.

"I know that, I was using a diminutive to indicate affection." She, uninvited, joined him. "I'm a very friendly person. Some fantastically wealthy and not at all bad-looking young heiresses are aloof. Not me. You know about what I'm heiress to?"

Sand replied, "probably the Sutt Soyball fortune."

"Tomhicky! You guessed it right off. That's double rosco." She twisted a finger in her blue hair, smiled and then laughed. "Yes, my daddy is C. Gillis Sutt, founder and president of Sutt Soyball, Ltd. We're the very biggest soybean junk food concern in the universe.

What takes me to Fumaza, if you're at all interested, is family business sort of."

"I'm not much interested." He tapped the base of his glass of mineral water.

"There are a heck of a lot of volcanoes on Fumaza. Were you aware of that?"

"Yep."

"Being volcanoes they erupt. Often with very wunky results." She paused to sip her ale. "One of the biggest ones erupted right smack in the middle of our largest soy plantation on Fumaza. Not only did it futz up endless acres of crops, it put hundreds of loyal field hands out of their homes. So I'm going to see about helping them."

"The beans or the workers?"

"Do you have a yen for me?"

"Not at all, nope."

"Oh, because you use the same nasty tone as you do when you talk to the Forbes girl," she said, "and her your top over tip in love with."

"Not actually."

"No, I'm very good at sensing these things. Like with my father, I knew way in advance when he was going gaga over his last three wives." She drank a bit more of her greenale. "Isn't that why you're on this tub at all, to pursue Glory Forbes?"

"This is a vacation."

"Don't be an ooze. Nobody in his right mind would head for Fumaza for fun," Barni said. "If I weren't bent on helping our poor displaced workers, I wouldn't go within a light-year of the dump. You think Fazenda was a sumphole, wait'll you set foot on this one. Makes Fazenda look like a resort satellite. They've got mewts on Fumaza that'll turn your . . . Yip! Better clear out, so as not to impede the course of true love." She popped to her feet, splashing a bit of green foam. "Hi, Glory."

"Barni." Glory had entered the small saloon and was walking directly over to Sand's table. "Must you hurry off?"

"I don't wish to be an ooze. Bye." She scooted away to the bar.

Glory took the vacated chair. "How much do you know?"

"About what?"

"Julia Brandywine."

"She's missing."

"C'mon, Sand," said the red-haired reporter. "You're not dealing with a dimwitted soy heiress now." She rested both elbows on the table. "This is getting much rougher than I anticipated going in and we, really, ought to pool what we know. I'd hate to see you end up dead?"

"Or even disabled?"

She shrugged her slim shoulders. "You'll note I didn't have them harm you, only your dichty android," she said. "I figured it would set you back some, but since you're heading out for Fumaza you must—"

"Did you get to Molly Yronsyde?"

Glory glanced away. "Let's just say I got hold of what information she had."

"Why not just do a piece about displaced soybean workers? Forget about the Brandywine business."

"Why don't you?"

"I'm being paid to—"

"So am I." She leaned closer. "Look, Sand, I know about Micro, know he's working on this, too, and that he's ahead of both of us. I think we really ought to beat him to the girl."

"There were three possible young women," said Sand,

eyes on her pretty face. "Each of them on a different Hellquad planet. How come you're going to Fumaza and not one of the others?"

"Same reason you aren't," she answered. "I found out that Micro's already been to the other two and is now en route to Fumaza. I deduced, same as you did, that he didn't find Julia on the other planets."

"Unless," he suggested, "Micro located her already and is only doing this to divert the competition."

She shook her head, red hair brushing at her shoulders. "Don't think so," she said. "He's not that subtle, nor that patient. If he had her, he'd be on his way to Barnum."

"Micro's already killed several people. You ought not to risk your life just for—"

"I'm going to Fumaza, you're going. That's already settled," she put in. "Let's move on to more practical stuff. If we team up we can beat Micro to—"

"Can't do that, Glory."

She leaned back in her chair. "What's that you're drinking?"

"Sparkling water."

"You never let down, do you?" She waved at the bartender.

"You want anything, lady, you got to haul your butt over here and fetch it," he called out. "We got no fancypants service on this tub."

Sand, slowly, got to his feet and grinned at the green man. "You'll make an exception in this case, though, won't you?"

"I'll stuff your . . . well . . . now that you mention it, okay." He kept his eyes from meeting Sand's again. "What'll it be, lady, and make it snappy."

"Earth whiskey on ice."

"Coming right up, lady."

Sand sat down again. "As I was saying, Glory, you and—"

"You really are an unsettling bastard," she told him. "I felt darn cold inside when you got up to stare that oaf down."

"Just a trick."

After the drink arrived Glory held the glass up toward Sand. "Cheers," she said, drinking down a third of it. "Have you thought about the Brandywines much?"

"Some."

"They're your clients, aren't they?"

"I'm working for Soldiers of Fortune, Inc."

"Sure," said Glory. "What do you think about the Brandywines. Were they spies?"

Sand asked, "What do you think?"

"I'm not certain. I've done, while getting prepared for this assignment, quite a bit of digging into the case," she said, rubbing her fingertips back and forth across the slick surface of the table. "Read, scanned, listened to a great lot of material about them. My first impression was that they were innocent, that they'd been railroaded."

"And now?"

"Okay, I can understand why you'd look for the daughter," she said. "I understand why I'm looking. But Micro and the PEO, that doesn't make much sense. They're not interested in seeing Julia Brandywine found and reunited with her loving parents. They'd only want her if the Brandywines had entrusted some valuable secret with her."

"Like one of the secrets they may have swiped back ten years ago."

"You know about Dr. Gobblinn, don't you?"

"Heard of him."

Both her hands circled her glass. "If there is a secret,

Sand, then it means the Brandywines are spies or worse," she said. "I don't understand how they could do that, take those risks, knowing they might be jailed or executed."

"People take risks like that all the time, Glory. Specially in fields that pay as well as spying sometimes does."

"Yes, but they had a daughter. She was a kid when they were doing this. They must've realized that if they were caught Julia'd be left alone. That she'd probably have her identity wiped away, be sent off Lord knows where."

"All parents," he said, "aren't splendid people."

"What were yours like?"

"Less than splendid." He stood. "I'm turning in, Glory."

"I wish you'd stay."

"Nothing else to talk about."

"I might want another drink and you're the only one who can get table service."

"Nevertheless." He grinned briefly, walked away from her.

Chapter 14

Sand eyed the thick plaz door of his cabin. Something had disturbed the tiny thread telltale he'd left on his door. Poking his tongue into his cheek, he glanced around the corridor.

There was no one else in sight.

He eased out his stungun with his right hand. With his left he silently turned the door handle.

Shoving the door suddenly open, he went diving into the room very low.

"... and Sacred Hooghly, rain blessings down on all the wretched sinners who ... Sir?" A red-bearded, green-suited missionary was kneeling beside Sand's bunk.

"Blessing my bedclothes, are you?"

"Eh?" The man was big, wide, with a sunbrowned face showing above his full whiskers. "I am here in my cabin, sir, in the midst of my nightly prayer to—"

"Birdshit," said Sand, indicating disbelief. "You've been searching my cabin, none too deftly."

The large man grunted to his feet. "Can I have been forgetful again and entered the wrong cabin?" He gave a puzzled look around the small disordered room. "Ah, though I pray to Hooghly near hourly to improve my feeble memory, yet I fear—"

"Take off the whiskers." Sand gestured with his stungun. "I just recognized you."

"Take them off, sir? Why, that violates one of the most sacred rules of my sect. For in his famous *Fifth Epistle to the Birdbath Makers*, Hooghly tells us, 'Awk! Awk! if a man shave his—' "

"No sermons just now, Typhoon."

The missionary scowled. "I didn't think you'd tumble so quick, Sand."

"Some people can wear false whiskers and some can't," he said. "I should've spotted you at dinner. Is the Reverend McManus one of your Political Espionage Office boys, too?"

"Naw, he's a really legitimate holy man," answered Typhoon Tyson. "For a substantial donation, he lets us pose as missionaries now and then."

"The other three holyrollers with PEO?"

"Just me this trip, Sand. We don't need a team to look after you and that Forbes bitch," he said. "I can do that and handle my job as well."

"Why's the PEO interested in Julia Brandywine?"

"We're not." He spread his hands wide. "Can I leave now? Sorry about messing up your—"

"Sit." He indicated a slingchair.

"Sand, you know damn well PEO regulations forbid any fraternizing with you."

"This won't remotely resemble fraternizing, Typhoon."

The big PEO agent shuffled his booted feet, looked at the floor, scratched at his red beard. "You sort of caught me in a darn awkward position and I ... I'm gonna massacre you!"

Tyson made a sudden lunge at Sand, intent on tackling him.

Sand, however, was no longer where he's been. Dodging, he avoided the charge entirely.

Zzzzzzummmmm!

The beam from his stungun took the agent in the ribs. He ran three awkward paces more, flapped his arms, dropped to his knees, fell sideways onto his red-whiskered face.

Sand stood watching him for a moment.

Putting his gun away, he rolled the PEO man over onto his back with his foot.

Tyson was unconscious, making low snoring noises.

Squatting, Sand frisked him. He found a stungun, a kilgun, a book entitled *Discourse On Birdseed & Other Sacred Writings* and a small flat PEO kit in a metal case. "Let's see if you gents have anything I haven't tried." Opening the kit, he scanned the contents. From it he selected a tiny sprayrod labeled *Truth Mist.* "Sounds interesting."

He dragged Tyson to the center of the cabin's linorug. Then sprayed a couple of whiffs of the gas at the agent's flat, wide nose.

"Tyson," he said after waiting a full minute. "Can you hear me?"

"Yes."

"Are you going to tell me the truth?"

"I am ... you bastard."

"Now, now. Let's keep personalities out of this." He settled into the sling chair. "What's your mission?"

"To find Julia Brandywine."

"Why?"

"We at PEO believe she's carrying the secret of Death 7."

"Carrying it how?"

"As a skullplant."

Sand rubbed at his chin. "You mean the information was transferred to a microdot and then inserted in her head by surgery?"

"Sure, that's what a skullplant is."

"Does she know it's there?"

"We believe not."

"So the Brandywines are spies after all."

"Hell, yes, Sand. We set this whole back-from-the-dead thing up to make them lead us to the secret."

"Why'd PEO wait ten years to do this?"

"We only found out about it recently. Nobody would've let the kid get away if we'd known back then," answered the mind-controlled agent. "And for a while there weapons like Death 7 were outlawed in the more civilized parts of the uni. Fortunately, times have changed and—"

"Who's Micro working for?"

"That little putz? We're not sure."

"What about the Brandywines themselves, are they on the hunt, too?"

"Not so far. You're doing their dirty work for them, you mercenary bastard."

"What about Glory Forbes?"

"She's too skinny for my tastes."

"I mean, who's she working for?"

"For the goddamn *Galactic Enquirer*. She's no secret agent, if that's what you mean."

"Why are you going to Fumaza?"

"Because that's where you're going, and where

Micro's going. Seems logical the Brandywine girl is there."

Sand was poking around in the kit again. "Limbolium," he said, holding up a vial. "What's that do, Typhoon?"

"Puts the subject into a deep trance for seventy-two hours (ESC)."

"What about the antidote?"

"We don't carry one with us. Limbolium is for using on subjects who are being shipped back to headquarters for various reasons."

"Something I can use." He selected a hypogun. "What's the dosage?"

"Three cc's."

"Okay." Sand filled the gun, left his chair and shot a dose into Tyson's left arm.

Chapter
15

A thick yellow fog hung over the spaceport, a fog that smelled strongly of sulfur and soot. There were few buildings and the passengers from the just landed *Space Queen* stepped from the disembark hatches directly into the open air. A good many of them began coughing and sniffling.

The foul air didn't bother Sand much. He stepped clear of the spacetramp, glanced around the port. It was not an impressive sight. Beyond their docking area stretched a flat patch of badly paved ground, cracked and weedy. There were probably black rocky hills surrounding the spaceport; you could make out vague hints of them through the fuzzy haze.

Circling the next dock over was a brass band, made up of lizard men and toadmen in bright crimson and gold uniforms. They were rendering an uplifting martial tune while a crowd of some fifty others yelled and waved signs and banners.

Welcome to the Hellquad Psy Olympics!
You Won't Beat Our Telek Team!
Hurrah For Precog Soccer!

Single suitcase in hand, Sand hurried across the foggy field to the row of six cardtables that had been set up by the Fumaza customs officials.

Before he reached them a skyambulance came wailing down out of the yellow sky.

"Oh, that poor missionary fellow," said a plump sneezing catwoman who was trotting along near Sand. "Going into a coma and missing all the fun."

"A pity, yes."

"I do hope it isn't contagious."

"No, I heard it was caused by some sort of mystic fervor."

"Well, you can catch most anything on these dreadful planets. That pushy girl reporter is ailing, too."

"What a shame."

"Yes, happened while we were breakfasting. She just up and passed out."

"Probably something she ate," said Sand, who'd arranged for knockout drops to be added to Glory Forbes morning juice.

"I wouldn't come near Fumaza except my youngest boy, Buttercup, is a high-placed executive with Sut Soyball. Perhaps you wonder why we call a grown catman Butter . . ."

Leaving the woman behind, Sand sprinted to the second table from the left. "Inspector Rius?"

The uniformed black man eyed him. "Mr. Sand?"

"Yep." He set his suitcase on the table, then handed over his ID packet.

Rius winked, smirked and commenced stamping the documents with a small stampgun. "You had an

ventful flight," he remarked. "An outbreak of plague
or one thing. We considered quarantining your ship."

"But you're not going to?"

When Rius shrugged the silvery fringe of his shoul-
er epaulets fluttered. "We decided one more plague
von't make much difference." He returned the packet
o Sand, winking again. "Have a pleasant stay on our
lanet, Mr. Sand, if that's possible."

"Thanks." Sand looked back at the Space Queen,
aw two white-suited medix hauling Typhoon Tyson
ut through a hatch on a stretcher. "That limbolium
vorks damn well."

At the edge of the field eleven landcabs were parked
n a row. Sand went to the third one from the right, a
right blue one.

"You Sargasso?" he asked the small, curly-haired
river.

"None other," he answered. "You are Sand?"

"Yep." He opened the rear door, tossed in his suit-
ase and eased in. "Let's head for the capital and an
ut of the way lodging house."

"Everything has been arranged. Your SOF friends
vere wise to hire Sargasso." He activated the engine,
ulled free of his slot and headed the cab away from
he field. "You'll find none so efficient, so reliable, so
ngratiating, so trustworthy. If you wish I'll provide
ou with a running commentary on the sights and
vonders we'll be passing."

"You can skip that. I'm not much in the mood for
vonders."

"Just as well, since you won't be awake to see any."
le punched three buttons on his dash.

"Whoa now, Sargasso. What—"

"Actually, sir, I am not Sargasso. And if you knew
argasso, you'd realize how happy that makes me."

A plaz partition had popped into place between Sand and the impostor driver. Up through small vents in the floor a pale green gas came whispering.

Sand grabbed at the door handle.

It wouldn't budge.

He intended to slam his shoulder against the door.

He passed out instead.

The earth shook.

The floor undulated, the plaz walls rattled.

Up above Sand, somewhere unseen, a sewdocrystal chandelier shivered and tinkled.

Sand opened his mouth, yawned. He blinked and noticed he was sprawled flat out on a thermorug with a pattern of twined purple leaves and vines.

There comes several more hollow rumbles. The walls rattled again, the floor did several hops beneath him.

"Frapping quakes ruin the reception," complained a gruff voice elsewhere in the room. "Volcano fumes don't help much either."

". . . time for the Hellquad's favorite satvid tellyshow, *Beggars Can't Be Choosers*. And here's our host, the man with a bundle of prizes to dole out to our wretched and woebegone contestants . . . Beano Gifford!"

Sand discovered he had to think about breathing, about sucking in air and expelling it again. He didn't seem to be very efficient at moving either. His initial attempts to rise were highly unsuccessful.

". . . c'mon, c'mon, you miserable welf," urged an impatient nasal voice from out the vidwall speakers. "Limp on over here into camera range, so we can get this fiasco on the road."

"Oh . . . Mr. Gifford, I'm so excited . . . being picked to be a contestant on *Beggars Can't Be Choosers* . . . La but it caused such a stir at the alms house where I—"

"Do I want to hear all this gab? Use those crutches of yours, granny, and get closer."

"I wonder . . . La, if I might have a kiss, Mr. Gifford. We watched your show every night on the vidwall . . . until our wall collapsed in the quake of—"

"Kiss you? Are you loony?"

"Well . . . you kiss a lot of the ladies."

"The pretty ones, granny, and the young ones. Not the wheyfaced old biddies like you. Gaw!"

"I'm only forty-one. It's working in the soy fields since I was a tyke that's—"

"And I suppose honest labor put all those unsightly purple blotches on your kisser, too?"

Sand made another try at rising. He got to his knees before collapsing flat out.

". . . okay, granny, are you ready to answer your first question?"

"La . . . I am . . . I may look old, but my mind's as sharp as a—"

"Before you prattle on anymore, here's Rollo to tell us what prize you'll win for a correct answer on the question."

"Right you are, Beano! The prize is . . . a crust of bread!"

"How about that, granny? Wouldn't you like to have a crust of bread for your very own?"

"La, I surely would, Mr. Gifford. We haven't had bread in the alms house since . . ."

Pushing hard against the floor with palms, Sand managed to rise to a hands and knees position.

". . . first question has to do with 19th Century Earth Literature, granny."

"That's not one of my strong subjects . . . but I'll do my level best, since I'd dearly love to win that bit of bread."

"Do me a favor, though, and don't wheeze into the mike . . ."

Pushing again, Sand managed to kneel.

The room he'd awakened in was large. The walls were of a gray pin-stripe pattern and the one-way glaz windows looked out on black night.

". . . sorry, granny, the correct answer is Henry Se ton Merriman."

"La, I almost said that."

"You have a chance at one more prize before we toss you out. Tell us about it, Rollo."

"Right you are, Beano. The prize for answering the next question correctly is a plyosack full of table scraps from one of the leading Venusian style restaurants on Fumaza!"

"La . . . what a feast that'd be for a starving wretch such as myself . . ."

Sand rose to his feet. Swayed. Dropped to one knee.

"Geeze, you take a flapping long time to come out of a simple gassing, buddy," said the apeman who was slouched in a hugchair near the vidwall. He was large, wide and wore a midnight-blue tuxsuit.

"One of my few weaknesses," Sand attempted to say. What came out was a dry mumble.

"Well, this ain't my favorite flapping show anyway." He turned off the wall, got up and lumbered over to pick up the voxphone. "He's awake." He listened, nodding, for a moment. "Yeah, sure. No flapping problem."

Sand took another look around the room. Except for the apeman's chair there was no furniture, nothing he could pick up and attack his guard with.

Not that he felt fully up to launching an attack anyway.

"Can you walk, buster?" the apeman asked him. "It'd save me the frapping trouble of carrying you."

"I can walk."

"Okay, then, come along," said the apeman. "Micro wants to talk to you."

                        green for these exertions. She confessed to
                        herself that her mission bothered

                        her at some time that the ...
                        ... neither pointing at the ...
                        other side of the wide table. "Do youse like
                        turkles?"

Chapter
16

Another quake struck just as Sand was pushed across
the threshold of the large, beam-ceilinged dining room.
The neowood-paneled walls produced low, whanging
sounds and all the glass and silverware on the sturdy
dining table rattled and tinkled.

The foot-high chromed jug sitting on the far end of
the table hopped twice, then once again. It came very
close to the table edge.

"Buffoon!" piped a high-pitched voice, amplified
from within the jug. "I almost took a nose dive."

"Youse must forgive me, boss." A huge man with
shoulder-length hair and a tight-fitting lemon yellow
tuxsuit bounced from his chair at midtable and,
carefully, slid the jug back to a safer spot on the crisp
white tablecloth.

"Your touch isn't deft, Strangler."

"Geeze, boss, you oughta consider that for a guy
with a moniker of Strangler I am damn gentle." He,

ossing his green hair in a disgruntled way, returned to his carved chair. "Da Sand bozo is here."

"I know that."

"Da boss wants youse should sit opposite me," informed Strangler Selznick, pointing at an empty chair on the other side of the wide table. "Do youse like wollo ala Jupiter?"

"Actually I'm more in the mood for fasting." Sand, launched by a push in the lower back from his apeman escort's paw, entered the dining wood and headed over to the table. "Evening, Micro."

"This is to be a gentlemanly meeting," said the jug. Sand sat down. "Oh, so?"

"Therefore you'll dine with us."

"Else I gotta break your arm maybe," said Strangler, smiling across at him. "And maybe tromp on your noggin."

"I'll dine," decided Sand. "What's the meeting about?"

"Address me, not that goon," said Micro from inside his jug.

"Why'd you highjack me?" Sand asked him.

"First . . . where's the first course of this alleged meal?" inquired Micro impatiently.

The apeman came into the room, shut the door and then tugged at a bellpull. "Cook's a little hard of hearing," he reminded. "Ever since you sat on her head, Strangler."

"Youse can't blame me for dat," the former wrestler said. "I found de old bimbo using margarine in a recipe that distinctly called for real groutbutter."

Sand rested an elbow on the table. "SOF isn't going to be happy about your kidnapping me out—"

"Elbows off the table," piped Micro.

"He don't like for his guests to be uncouth."

Sand left his arm where it was. "Look, let's quit the games," he said, at the glistening jug. "Tell me why the hell you had me brought here and why—"

"Gentlemen never discuss business until after dinner."

"Since neither of us is a gentleman, that needn' bother us, Micro."

"Youse is a wiseacre," observed Strangler, massaging one meaty fist with the huge fingers of the other.

"Although we've never met before, Sand," said Micro, "I have heard a good deal about—"

"Mercy me, why all the gongs going off in my scullery?" A large catwoman in a printed frock and a large white apron had come tottering in through a swinging side door.

"Da boss wants that youse should start slinging the hash, ya old crow."

"What's that?" She cupped a calico paw to a calico ear.

"CHOW!" boomed Strangler. "YOUSE CAN SERVE DE DAMN FIRST COURSE!"

"Oh, mercy me, that's going to take some time yet." She hid her paws beneath her ample apron. "Have you ever tried getting grouttail soup in an eyedropper?"

"Dat's how we gotta put food into da boss' jug," explained Strangler to Sand, leaning both his massive elbows on the table.

"Manners, Strangler, manners."

"Geeze, I'm sorry, boss." He whisked his elbows off, rubbing at them.

"Tell Mrs. Malley to serve the soup course to you two," instructed Micro. "I'll pass."

"Aw, youse oughtn't to skip da soup, boss," cautioned Strangler. "You know what Dr. Coulton says in his *Teenie Weenie Diet Book*. Even small people got to get a well-balanced—"

"Tell her to bring in the soup!"

"SERVE THE GODDAMN SOUP, MRS. M!"

"Very well. To hear is to obey." Turning, she went hobbling out of the room.

"Sand," asked Micro, "what brings you to Fumaza."

"Business."

"You believe she's here, don't you?"

Sand slouched some in his straightback chair. "I imagine you think the missing Brandywine girl is here, too."

"She wasn't on Farpa. That possible candidate was not Julia Brandywine," said the jug. "What a rotten planet that was, nothing but sand and bums."

"Da broad wasn't the one on Farridor neither," added Strangler. "We queried the supposed dame real good."

"What about your candidate on this planet?" Sand asked the green-haired man.

"Don't keep directing your questions to him," said Micro. "Talk to me, Sand."

"Well?" Sand turned toward the silvery jug.

"As you know, a young woman, one of the three answering the general description of the missing Julia Brandywine, was reported to be working on the planet Fumaza under the name Jill Bowker. She traveled, in the capacity of something called a daredevil groutrider, with a flybynight circus calling itself Colonel Bob's All Star Circus & Mudwrestling Extravaganza."

"You can't find her?"

"We found da colonel," answered Strangler. "He's a rumdum old coot, residing in Tenderloin #6 right here in the city of Caldera."

"He doesn't know where the young woman went to," said Micro.

"Nope, he really didn't," confirmed Strangler. "When you apply a wolloprodder to dere goonies, they tell youse everything."

Sand frowned in the direction of the jugged Micro. "When's the last time he saw her?"

"Nearly three years ago."

"Where'd she go?"

Micro chuckled. "I am operating on the assumption that you know the answer to that, Sand," he replied. "According to the colonel they were touring the provinces . . . for the life of me I don't know how you can distinguish the provinces from the metropolises on a backward planet such as this . . . at any rate, the young woman was with the show one day and gone the next. She vanished completely and we have been unable to find a single trace of her."

Strangler's green hair fluttered as he nodded and smiled across at Sand. "We want youse should tell us where the broad is."

Sand had been feeling increasingly unusual for the past few minutes. Possibly it was an aftereffect of being gassed and abducted. He felt himself growing more and more aware of his circulatory system. His veins seemed to be tingling, burning, sizzling. His head was commencing to throb.

"Mr. Sand?" said Micro impatiently.

"Hum?"

"I want to know where the young woman is," said Micro.

"And youse must know or youse wouldn't of come here."

"What I intended to do . . ." He paused, shook his head. It felt as though it was filling up with hot water, or maybe grouttail soup "I . . . intended to look . . ."

All at once Sand felt as though a giant hand were clutching him, squeezing the air out of him and yanking him free of his chair.

The dining room went snapping away; darkness took hold of him.

Chapter
17

He was face to face with Queen Victoria.

Her plump countenance showed nothing but disapproval. "We are not amused . . ." she said before her rusty voice wound down to silence.

Sand, shaking his head, took a step backward.

"Have a care, sir," advised William Makepeace Thackeray.

Sand was slightly dizzy and a pain had developed low in his back. He'd been, somehow, transported from the dining room at Micro's temporary villa to what appeared to be the back room of a shutdown Eminent Victorians Pizza Theater. He was curious as to why.

"Hoy! Sargasso's Cousin Carlos excelled. He did a better job than even Sargasso anticipated, landing you smackdab on the spot."

Turning slowly, Sand found himself confronting a small curly-haired man in a two-piece white funsuit. "You're the real Sargasso?"

"Need you ask?" He spread his arms wide, did a slow revolving turn, nearly bumped into an android Florence Nightingale. "Are there tha⁺ many on this blighted planet half so handsome and compact?"

"Probably not. How'd you get me here?"

"Look down," suggested Sargasso, chuckling.

Doing so, Sand noted a large X chalked on the neowood planks of the floor. "So?"

"Sargasso drew that mark, instructed his Cousin Carlos and . . . Zam!"

Sand glanced around the shadowy room. "Where's Carlos?"

"In the vicinity of Micro's foul lair, of course. That's how teleportation works, at least Cousin Carlos' brand. He needs must be close to the object rather than the delivery target."

"Carlos is a telek?"

"All the Sargasso clan is gifted, in various unique and admirable ways." Sargasso smiled, head bobbing. "Cousin Carlos happens to be a champion teleporter, here for the Psi Olympics, of which you've no doubt heard. When I explained to him that I needed to rescue a client from the clutches of—"

"Why didn't you meet me at the spaceport, the way SOF intended?"

"Hoy!" Because Micro caused me to be waylaid, sewed up in a gunnysack and sunk in the sacred waters of the Sister Ursula Lagoon on the outskirts of town," answered Sargasso. "Were it not for the fact I had been taught the secrets of escape by my cousin Sargasso the Great, one of the foremost magicians in the—"

"How'd you know where I'd been taken?"

"Zam! Isn't Sargasso a crackerjack operative?"

"Is he?"

"I am," confirmed Sargasso. "Why are you wincing? Do you mistake my honest faith in myself for bragging or—"

"Developing a backache. Probably from being gassed, shoved around by an apeman and teleported."

"Could also be an allergic reaction," said Sargasso, rubbing the tip of his nose. "The mold and pollen count is terrible today. Are you hungry?"

"Not particularly."

"Even though this restaurant is shut, due to a complete lack of interest in both belles lettres and pizza in this lowbrow neighborhood, the cooking facilities are still functioning. Using skills taught me by my Cousin Tamisa, who conducted a very highly rated cooking show on satvid before running off with her greengrocer, I am able to whip up at least seventeen kinds of pizza. Grout and anchovies, wollo and mushrooms, snerg and—"

"No thanks," cut in Sand. "How come we're here at all?"

"Sargasso is, as you may have noted, something of a mystery man. He has, therefore, lairs and dens all over Caldera and other major cities on Fumaza. This is one such hideaway, a bistro owned by my Cousin Filipe."

Rubbing at his lower back, Sand said, "Micro grabbed me because he's come to a dead end in his hunt for the girl called Jill Bowker. How about you?"

"Zam! Sargasso never hits dead ends." He drew himself up, chest out. "What we're in now is more an impasse and by morning we'll be back on the trail."

"Meantime I'd like to clean up someplace, maybe rest up a few hours."

"Sargasso has already anticipated that. I've arranged quarters on a houseboat owned by my Cousin Luis. You have no objections to dwelling on the water?"

"None. How do we get there?"

"Well, we can wait for Cousin Carlos to return and teleport us there," said Sargasso, "or we can hire a landcab."

Sand massaged his back. "Let's take a cab."

His cabin rocked gently from side to side. In through the small open porthole came rays of bright morning sunshine, along with swirls of yellowish sulfurous smoke and the strong stench of the river.

Sand sat up in the plyohammock, stretched and discovered the pain in his back wasn't as bad as it'd been last night.

"Breakfast in bed is impossible," said Sargasso as he came into the cabin, "in a hammock. Therefore I'm preparing a repast to be served out on deck."

Swinging to the floor, Sand noticed that the curly-haired field op was keeping his left hand behind his back. "Hiding something?"

"Does defeat and frustration affect your appetite? If so, Sargasso will withhold the—"

"Tell me now."

Sargasso produced a faxpaper tabloid from behind him and flourished it. "Behold the latest edition of the *Galactic Enquirer*, hot off the faxprinter."

Scanning the major headline, Sand said, " 'Mud-wrestler Loses 40 Pounds In 6 Days! You Can Do The Same!' Why would that unsettle me or—"

"This is the yarn that'll do it." He held the paper higher, pointed to a red headline. " 'Lost Brandywine Daughter Found! *Enquirer* Reporter Locates Her!' Does that whisk away your desire for breakfast?"

Sand went striding across the cabin, grabbed the tabloid. "Story on Page Three," he said and opened the paper. "That damn Glory Forbes beat us all to the . . ." Folding the newspaper back to the right page, he dropped into a canvas slingchair and started reading the full-page account. " '. . . gorgeous titian-haired reporter . . . overcoming incredible odds . . . attempts on life . . . locates missing Julia Brandywine . . . living in quiet seclusion on Fumaza . . .' Damn!"

"Just about under our noses the girl's been, in fact."

Sand glanced up. "Hum?"

"Note the photo of the prodigal daughter." Sargasso moved to Sand's side and pointed.

The young woman was sitting on a terrace with her back to the camera. You couldn't see her face at all, but out beyond the terrace you got an impressive view of a smoldering volcano. "You recognize the mountain?"

"Even an eye far less than Sargasso's would. It's Mount Branco, less than fifty miles from here."

"The story doesn't seem to say exactly where Julia is, but using that mountain as a landmark we—"

"We and Micro and Typhoon Tyson," said Sargasso.

Frowning, Sand returned to reading Glory Forbes' report on the finding and interviewing of Julia Brandywine. When he reached the middle of the story, his frown deepened. "Girl says, 'The mindwipe they used on me wasn't a very good one apparently. My real memories started coming back about five years ago. Within a few months I remembered everything, knew who I really was. Once I realized I was Julia Brandywine, I began looking into my background and that of my parents. I read, scanned, listened to a great deal of material about them. My first impression was that they were innocent, that they'd been railroaded.' Damn."

"You doubt the young lady's word?"

Sand skimmed the rest of the story. "A lot of what she says I've heard before."

"Where?"

"From Glory Forbes." He stood, dropping the tabloid in the slingchair.

"Journalists frequently put their own words into the mouths of their interviewees," Sargasso said.

"That damn picture is goofy, too," said Sand. "The girl could be anybody."

"She may not wish to be recognized by the gawking masses."

"Sure, she's hiding out and living in deep seclusion, yet she allows a photo that just about pinpoints her hideaway." He started to pace.

"Zam! You don't think the estimable Glory Forbes has stooped to journalistic faking?"

"Nope, Glory doesn't work that way. She'd break your leg to keep you from beating her to a story, but . . These have to be real quotes from Julia Brandywine and a real picture of her . . . Except . . ." Crossing the cabin, he stepped out onto the deck.

Several fat pink gulls were squabbling over garbage that floated and bobbed just off the stern of the houseboat.

"Are we," inquired Sargasso as he followed Sand, "to do the obvious thing and locate that house in the shadow of Mount Branco?"

"We're going to be a bit less obvious," Sand told him, "and locate Glory Forbes."

Chapter
18

The librarian whispered, "Hit the deck!"

Seconds later the glaz window over the library desk Sand was using exploded inward. Several brix and a few stray sprays of subdumist came flying into the reading room.

By that time Sand had grabbed the mapscanner and dived under the table with it.

"Scoot over," requested the librarian as she made her way to the desk on hands and knees. She was a handsome silver blonde woman of around thirty.

Sand, lifting the mapscanner onto his lap, made room. "What sort of trouble is going on out there?"

Another few brix whizzed in from the street, clattering on the desk top above them.

"Geeze, I hope too much of that subdumist the cops are using doesn't come spritzing in here," the blonde librarian said. "Last time this happened I got a rea snootful, became so docile I let a Venusian dockwalloper with warts into my bed."

"These things happen often?"

"This branch of the Caldera Public Library, see, is right across from the Federal Dole offices, which means there's always something doing. Today it's mostly zekes."

"Zekes?"

"Don't they have zekes where you come from?"

"Don't know. Give me a few more hints, Trixie."

Trixie Flame explained, "Zekes are like welfs, only crummier. A welf is a no good who won't work and lives off welfare. When the dole runs out for him on one planet, a welf bums a ride to another and starts all over with the freeloading."

"That I know."

"Okay, a zeke used to be a welf, but he's been reclassified as being of zero economic worth. A zeke."

"Meaning what?"

"He doesn't get any more welfare, because he's beyond hope of ever being taken back into the workaday world anywhere on the Hellquad," said Trixie. "Naturally, being lazy lunks, zekes get ticked off about their dole being cut off and, every now and again, they stage a riot. Such as this one."

"Do the riots last long?"

"Usually takes the cops about an hour to subdue one and get everybody hauled away."

Nodding, Sand turned his attention again to the pale green screen of the library mapreader. He'd been, since Sargasso introduced him to Trixie and departed over an hour ago, going over maps of the area around Mount Branco.

Trixie asked, "You an old chum of Sargasso?"

"Not exactly."

"He's a swell guy. He's admired me for several years," she said. "Not as a woman, but as an artist."

Sand pushed the enlarge button. Less than five miles from Mount Branco, according to this map, was a Redbearded Hooghly Brotherhood Monastery. If Mailorder McManus could be bought by Typhoon Tyson, might he be for sale to Glory Forbes? Sand had a hunch she wouldn't be staying at the house shown in the Enquirer photo, but at someplace else nearby. A location from which she could watch the house and keep up with who visited it.

". . . a Zero-G stripper," Trixie was saying. "Torrid Trixie Flame I was known as then. I dropped the Torrid when I undertook this library stint because . . ."

He reactivated the rollerscan. "Damn." He halted it, jabbed the enlarge button once more.

This map was supposedly only weeks old and it showed a new facility less than three miles from the base of the volcano. A Sutt Soyball Relocation Center. Barni Sutt had been on the spacetramp coming out here to Fumaza. Could she be in cahoots with Glory, letting her use the center as a hideout? And would a muckraker like Glory have anything to do with agricultural exploiters like the Sutts?

". . . nothing but feathers, you understand? There I am, suspended in air, gracefully plucking these feathers from my person one by one. It drove the audiences wild. One evening a delegation of birdmen from . . ."

Sand devoted another ten minutes to consulting the map, but noticed nothing else of interest.

"All clear," said Trixie, crawling free from under the desk.

"Hum?"

"Riot's over. Careful you don't step on glaz getting out from there."

He eased up, replaced the mapscanner on the desk top.

Fragments of glaz gleamed on the desk top, on the thermorug and on several of the bookfiche cabinets. The elderly catman who'd been reading the cartoon bible had apparently taken in too strong a whiff of subdumist and was now dozing over the large book. There were quite a few brix underfoot.

Trixie was still brushing dust and lint from her skirt when Sargasso came striding in.

"Hoy! The obtuseness of the police," he remarked. "A minion of the law actually mistook me for a zeke and, had I not been able to glibly persuade him otherwise, would've herded me into the wagon and—"

"Find out anything?" Sand guided him over into a litscanner alcove.

"Typhoon Tyson has recovered," replied Sargasso, "and at last report was speeding in the general direction of Mount Branco."

"And Micro?"

"Left the villa at dawn, exact destination as yet undetermined. I'm betting he's moving for the vicinity of the volcano, too."

"Anything else?"

"Are you two zanies going to gab all the livelong day?" inquired a toadman in the next alcove. "I'm trying to pursue a lively interest in 19th Century Earth Literature and, I mean, the distractions have been horrendous. First, I mean, it's a bunch of welfare freeloaders rioting in the streets and then it's the pair of you blabbing away to beat the band and, I mean, I'm all wrapped up in the plight of Mr. Midshipman Easy and—"

"We'll step to another alcove."

"Not bad enough I get hit on the coco with not one but two brix and almost . . ."

In an alcove nearer the far wall Sand asked, "Find out anything else?"

"Sargasso came up with one other item," he said. "This ought to interest you. The Brandywines, Hazel and Jonas, are at this very moment enroute for this very planet."

"Who told you that, Soldiers of Fortune, Inc?"

"SOF," Sargasso informed him, "doesn't know a damn thing about it."

Twilight was spreading through the jungle, the smoky air grew even darker.

Sargasso turned on the headlights of their landcar. "You have to admit that Sargasso's Cousin Raoul has excellent taste in vehicles," he said as he steered the maroon car along the jungle roadway. "The ride over all these tedious miles has been smooth, comfortable—"

"Can't hear you over all this rattling and bumping." Sand was hunched in the passenger seat.

"Would you like to hear some classical music maybe? The sound reproducing equipment in this buggy is impressive. Once you've heard the Farpa All Lizard Pops Symphony Orchestra play something like Ferman's 'Just About Finished Symphony,' you've experienced—"

"How much longer before we get to the Sutt Soyball hangout?"

"Hoy! You really must learn to appreciate life's every minute," advised Sargasso. "We've been driving through highly scenic surroundings, reveling in each other's company, yet you don't seen to enjoy—"

"Reveling may not be the best word to describe my feelings."

"It's your back. Even while reclining on the luxurious groutskin upholstery, your injured buttocks are—"

"Didn't injure my buttocks. The pain is a shade higher up."

"There's a whirlpool bath under the back seat, did I mention? Why not slip back there, submerge your aching frame in—"

"How much farther?"

"Less than five miles. Having learned to drive from my cousin I . . . Zang!"

Sand sat up. "What?"

Sargasso was glancing from side to side, scanning the darkening road and the high trees on either side. "Did you happen to notice a handsome suntanned blond chap darting among the trees a few seconds ago?"

"Nope. Odd spot for a hitchhiker."

"It might've been an alfie."

Narrowing his eyes, Sand stared out into the darkening day. "That's another local type I'm not up on."

"Alfie stands for artificial life form," explained Sargasso. "Did you happen to take note of that large defunct factory we roared by while exiting the town? No matter, that was the alfie plant. Been closed for several years, ever since the alfies ran away."

"What are they, androids?"

"No, synthetic men, grown in the factory with artificial genes and such in special tanks." Sargasso shook his curly head. "The whole project was ill-advised. Imagine thinking that people would want to have big blond louts in servant and menial capacities. Had they designed their alfies to be rather on the short side, with tight-curling raven locks then . . . Zam! they'd have had something marketable."

"Besides the design error," asked Sand, "what else went wrong?"

"They built in too much vanity and independence.

The alfies refused to work, maintaining it was beneath them. They staged a revolt and most of them ran off, settling in these very jungles."

"What do they do for a living?"

"They prey on wayfarers. They're highwaymen."

"Then that explains," said Sand, "why five of them have just popped up on the road ahead armed with kilguns."

Chapter
19

Sargasso punched a red button on the dash. "Nothing to fear, this baby's equipped to repel boarders."

More alfies, each and every one big, blond and bronzed, were popping out of the jungle on all sides of the maroon landcar.

The car made a tired whining noise, a tiny light next to the red button commenced blinking. "You neglected your last 10,000 mile checkup," said a metallic schoolmarmish voice, "and aren't you sorry now? Your stunbeams are rundown."

"Zang!" Sargasso, keeping the car rolling straight at the alfies in its path, jabbed at a green button. "We'll use the auxiliary stunners on these lunkheads."

"Now you're seeing the folly of faulty maintenance practices, aren't you?" said the voice of the dash. "The auxiliaries are on the fritz, too."

Sand had his stungun in his hand. "Keep this crate moving. They'll get out of our way."

"I'm not sure that—"

Thump!

Their car collided with the first handsome alfie.

Thump!

Thunk!

"Did I mention they have no fear of death?"

"I was coming to that conclusion."

Dozens of suntanned blond young men were crowding the roadway ahead of them, each carrying a kilgun.

"We're slowing down," said Sargasso. "I can't make much headway with this many louts strewn in our path."

"Just so we keep moving some."

Blond alfies were surrounding the car, staring handsomely in at them. Every single one of them wore a spotless three-piece white cazsuit.

"Hoy! They're really impeding our progress."

"Roughly how many of them are there?"

"Nobody's quite certain. Originally about fifteen hundred of them broke free of the factory," said Sargasso. "I wonder if the windshield wipers'll swat a few of them away."

The alfies were swarming up on the hood, on the roof, all over the barely moving car.

"Never seen so many perfect teeth in my life," observed Sand. "Originally fifteen hundred, how many now?"

"There's a theory these pretty boys've learned how to replicate themselves," answered Sargasso. "Meaning there may well be untold thousands of them lurking in there amid the flora and fauna."

Sand hunched his shoulders. "We're not moving much at all."

"I ought to have recalled that Cousin Raoul is negligent about the upkeep of this handsome machine. Sometimes he's so thoughtless he even forgets to put in a new fuel cell when the old one is near to—"

Runkle! Rumble!

Fitz! Sput!

"This," said Sand, "is apparently one of those times."

Their landcar stopped entirely.

"Zam! How can a man with Sargasso blood in his veins and Sargasso gray matter in his skull be such a hopeless twit?"

"A more interesting question," said Sand," is how do we shake the alfies? Are they noted for their patience?"

"They'll stick to our car until we come out," said Sargasso. "We can't, if that's what you're contemplating, sit them out. They might even decide to dismantle our jalopy and get at us that way."

"We've goth got stunguns. We can try to clear a path through them, get away from here on foot."

"Stunning a few hundred golden-haired alfies isn't going to be the easiest of tasks."

"Suggest an alternate."

"Sargasso's fabled brain is even now racing through possible schemes, weighing the merits and drawbacks of each."

"What do alfies do with their victims?"

Sargasso scratched at his curly hair. "I really can't answer that too well, mostly because so few of their victims ever show up again."

Sand tapped the window on his side with the barrel of his stungun. "We might as well try to shoot our way through," he said. "All this handsomeness is starting to unsettle me."

Alfies were everywhere outside, cutting off the view

of the early night jungle, pressing close to the stalled car and staring in with their tan faces blank.

"Sargasso must really be sinking in your esteem. Allowing this pack of blond dolts to delay us on our . . . Zam!" He cocked his head, listening.

From some distance off a strange wailing cry had sounded.

It was repeated, closer, a moment later.

Expressions suddenly started appearing on the alfies' bland faces. Eyebrows rose, mouths dropped open.

"Something's scaring them," said Sand.

Sargasso chuckled, rubbed his hands together. "They're frightened of Lorna the Jungle Girl."

"That's her producing that yowling?"

"It's her battle cry, sort of."

The alfies were dropping off the car. Stumbling, uneasiness and fright showing on their handsome identical faces, they started to push their way into the surrounding jungle.

In less than five minutes the stalled car sat alone on the road.

Lorna coughed into her pudgy fist. "Boy, I sure wish I could kick this habit," she said, nodding at the cigarette in her other hand. "Smoking really slows you up. I swing through no more than a half dozen trees these days and I'm wheezing like a sick accordion. And did you catch my jungle yell, Sargasso?"

"It sounded splendid to us," he assured her.

"Aw, can the malarkey. It sounded like a sick cat getting stepped on. I just don't have the wind anymore." She shook her head, her graying hair fluttering. "The days when I could send chills to the hearts of the jungle denizens are long gone."

"You sure scared off the alfies," Sargasso reminded.

"Those pansies. You can say, 'Boo!' and scatter them."
She eyed Sand. "But you haven't introduced me to
your pal here."

The three of them were standing beside the landcar.

"I'm John Wesley Sand." He held out his hand.

Lorna took a puff of her cigarette, coughed, shook
hands. "Pleased to meet you," she said. "I'm Lorna the
Jungle Girl. At least I used to be."

Sargasso said, "What kind of talk is that, Lorna?"

She smoothed the blue animal skin she wore as a
dress, took a drag of the cigarette. "I been at this a hell
of a long time." She turned to Sand. "How old would
you guess I am, John?"

"Fifty."

Lorna sighed. "See, Sargasso? Here I am barely forty-
three and your buddy pegs me at fifty."

"No doubt," said Sargasso, "it's the rough life you
lead, Lorna. Out in the open all the time, swinging
from limb to limb in the lofty trees, fighting with
wild beasts of every sort, keeping peace among the
diverse denizens of the jungle. Makes for a stressful
life."

"If it's so stressful, how come I'm thirty-one pounds
overweight?"

"Exercise isn't everything. Mayhap your diet is—"

"Bananas," said Lorna. "I live just about entirely on
bananas and other fruit. Still keep putting on the
pounds." She inhaled smoke. "If I ever quit smoking,
I'd probably really balloon up."

"Be that as it may," said Sargasso, "we want to
thank you for shooing off the alfies."

She shrugged. "Think nothing of it," she said. "Say,
Sargasso, what would you think if I was to change my
name?"

"To what?"

"From Lorna the Jungle Girl to Lorna the Middle-aged Jungle Woman."

"Nay," said Sargasso. "That lacks zing."

"But a gray-haired, dumpy jungle girl isn't—"

"You'll always be the jungle girl in the hearts of your myriad admirers."

Lorna puffed on her cigarette, exhaled smoke, then kissed Sargasso on the cheek. "That's what I like about you, Sargasso. You tell a lady the sort of thing she wants to hear."

Sand tapped the hood of their landcar. "Suppose we see if we can get this thing rolling once again."

Lorna asked, "Listen, are you two guys in a big rush?"

"We're on a rather important mission," admitted Sargasso. "Why?"

She dug her big toe into the sward. "Aw, it's a sort of routine job I've been putting off. Since I have you two palookas here, I thought you could maybe lend me a hand. A rescue thing."

Sand asked, "What sort of rescue?"

"Part of my duties," Lorna explained, "include rescuing young ladies from the clutches of the International Brotherhood of Pimps, Panderers and Slavers, Local 232. They use my jungle as a base every so often. I run them off, they sneak back."

"They've grabbed someone?"

"Pretty thing, too. Tall, slim, red-haired. Wish I had a waist like that again ... I saw them do it and I should've rescued her right then but ... well, you know, when you get up into your forties ... especially when you *look* fifty ... you start hesitating, putting off. Now I like to make sure I've got just the right rescue scheme worked out before I go up against a band of slavers—"

"A red-haired young woman?" Sand took hold of her bare arm. "When was this?"

"Only yesterday. The poor kid was staying at the Soyball center, went for a stroll in the jungle and ten of the scummiest slavers you ever laid eyes on 'umped—"

"We'll help you," said Sand.

Chapter 20

Wheezing, Lorna called a halt. She rested her hand against the bole of a thick yellow tree, lifted her left foot. "Sometimes I wish they'd paved this damn jungle," she said as she massaged her instep.

They had trekked through the jungle for several hours, halted for a rest and then resumed their march toward the slavers' enclave. The night was slowly giving way to dawn, the smoky air was turning gradually lighter.

"No doubt you'd move more swiftly alone," said Sargasso when they started walking again. "Swinging gracefully from sturdy branch to . . . Hoy!" He slowed, gazing up into the tangle of branches high above him. "What's that strange blond creature dangling up there?"

"Nothing, never mind," said Lorna, taking several quick puffs at her cigarette. "Let's keep going."

"Just hanging there on that branch, it somewhat resembles a wig."

"It is a wig. Forget it."

"Yours?"

"I gave way to vanity, Sargasso, thought I might appear more youthful that way. So I bought myself a half dozen, darn expensive wigs," admitted the middle-aged jungle girl. "Trouble was, it's awful hard to keep a wig on while swinging through the trees. I lost every damn one of the things."

Sand, who was bringing up the rear, asked, "About how much farther to the slavers, Lorna?"

She took a deep breath before replying. "Another couple miles is all, John. Gee, I wish I had some guy as anxious over finding me as you are over this redhead."

"This isn't," said Sand, "a romantic quest exactly."

"Aw, go on. I know a guy who's carrying a torch when I see one."

They trudged on in silence for several minutes.

Lorna finished her cigarette, snuffed it out. "We'll be seeing the lost city soon as we get over that rise up ahead."

"Lost city? Zang! I'm a great lost city buff. Ancient ruins, the once mighty remains of a long vanished civilization," said Sargasso. "The vegetation reclaiming the aging stones of what used to be—"

"Relax, Sargasso," she told him while lighting a fresh cigarette. "This city only got lost six years ago."

"Eh?"

"Part of a government boondoggle," Lorna explained. "They started to build out here, claiming it would revitalize the jungle and turn it into a thriving residential and commercial area. The idea didn't catch on, though, and what you'll find here in the middle of the wilderness is just six square blocks of office, municipal and apartment buildings.

"Hoy." Sargasso shook his head. "That's not my idea of a lost city or—"

"Quiet a minute," suggested Sand, glancing back over his shoulder.

"It's part of my character to wax enthusiastic over—"

"Yep, but control it. I hear something." Sand eased out his stungun.

Lorna coughed. "Me, too. Should've noticed earlier, what with my keen wilderness senses and all. I guess this damn smoking habit really dulls—"

"Hush," said Sand.

The chuffing of a motor could be heard, indicating some sort of land vehicle was moving toward them along the trail they'd been traveling.

"Landjeep," guessed Sargasso, "from the sound of it."

"Okay, we'll fan out into the brush," said Sand. "If it's an enemy, wait for my signal—"

"Who else could it be but an enemy?" Sargasso had his stungun out. "We don't have that many chums in this area."

Sand sprinted across the trail, ducked down behind a thorny flowering bush and waited.

The noise of the approaching vehicle grew louder. Then a yellow landjeep came rolling into view.

The jeep stopped directly in front of Sand's bush.

"One doesn't like to be overly critical, especially at a moment of sentimental reunion," said Munson, leaning out. "Yet I must point out that even an unsophisticated tyke couldn't fail to take note of you behind the foliage there, sir."

Lorna put a restraining arm around Sargasso. "Relax," she urged. "Don't let him rile you."

"Nobody can dub Sargasso a halfpint." He struggled o get a chance to punch the newly arrived android.

"You'll only bust your fingers," cautioned the jungle girl. "He's made of metal and plaz."

"Ha! The Sargassos don't know the meaning of ear."

"One imagines that is the first in a long list of things hey do not know." Munson was standing beside his halted jeep.

"Enough," said Sand.

The android rubbed the tips of his gloved fingers ogether. "I anticipated finding you in low company, ir, since there is little else on any of the Hellquad planets," he remarked. "Yet these two are even lower han I—"

Bonk!

"Hoy!" Sargasso had broken free and planted a kick on the android's shin. He was hopping around on the rail now, holding his hurt toes.

"Suppose," said Sand, "you explain what you're doing here, Munson."

"Where else ought one to be?"

"I left you in Gonzaga's workshop on Fazenda."

"Ah, that seems eons ago," said Munson. "He wasn't a bad technician and, with many a useful suggestion rom me, the repair work was completed in jig time. Once back on my feet again, I naturally set off to track you and resume my duties." He bowed in Sand's lirection.

"You found me without much trouble."

Munson rubbed the side of his sharp nose with his forefinger. "One hesitates to take credit for abilities nstalled in one at your behest, sir," he said modestly. "Yet I am an excellent tracker. And that bug planted on your body, once I became aware of it, made the work even easier than—"

"Bug?" Sand slapped at his back. "That's why I've had a sore spot. That god damned Micro implanted a tracking device on me."

"Zam!" lamented Sargasso.

"He's been trailing us all this time," said Sand, "while we lead him directly to Glory Forbes."

"One would think that didn't much matter, since it's actually Julia Brandywine we are—"

"Can you deactivate this damn gadget," asked Sand, "until I have time to get it removed?"

"Most certainly." Stroking the glove from his left hand, Munson reached around and touched Sand's lower back with his thumb.

Zzzzzzitttzzzzz!

"There you are, sir." He smiled, put his glove back on. "One might mention that, had you not abandoned one to the ministrations of Gonzaga and instead waited until one was shipshape again, the implantation of that rather crude device would have been detected much earlier in the game. Instead of roaming jungly wilds with these tacky nomads you—"

"I'm no nomad!" Sargasso attempted another kick.

"Cease all this." Sand stepped between the android and the curly-haired op. "We've got to get Glory free from these slavers before Micro catches up with us."

"Do you have a plan for effecting the young journalist's rescue, sir?" inquired Munson. "One refrains from even asking why you're wasting time over a person who's been a thorn in your side from the very outset of this—"

"Now that you're here, Munson," cut in Sand, "we won't have to sneak up on these guys."

"Hoy!" said Sargasso. "How are we going to get her out of there then?"

"You and Lorna'll stay here and watch out for Micro," answered Sand. "Munson and I'll go into their headquarters and buy her from the slavers."

Chapter 21

The buildings of the lost city stood shrouded in fog and smoke.

"One realizes that the pickings on these woebegone planets are slim," said Munson as he drove the landjeep onto the main street. "Yet those two fatheads back there are—"

"Concentrate on the matter at hand."

The streets of the six-block city were cracked, taken over by weeds, roots and vines. The public fountain in the civic square was dry and a small young palm tree had come pushing up through the flagstones beside it.

Seated on the rim of the dead fountain were two lizard man pimps. They wore electric blue two-piece funsuits, widebrim orange hats, wraparound rose-tinted glasses and considerable glittering gold jewelry. Each had a blasterifle resting across his knees.

"Park near those two dazzling lizard lads," instructed Sand.

"You actually wish to get within range of them?"

"How else can we do business?"

The pimp guards jumped to their yellow-booted feet, rifles pointing at the approaching jeep.

"Hold it right there, daddy," ordered one of them.

"Ignore him, park next to the fountain."

"One complies, refraining from comment on the foolhardy—"

"You just play this the way I told you, Munson." The jeep came to a smooth halt and Sand stepped clear. "I like your style, fellas. Don't trust anybody."

"We sure don't trust you, dude." The taller lizard man prodded him in the ribs with his rifle. "You better have one hell of a good reason for your butt being here or—"

"Surely you're expecting us?" Sand began to frown, glancing back at Munson in a puzzled way.

"Why should we be expecting a scrawny gink and a pommy andy?"

"I'm the rep from Moms Goodtime. You people were supposed to be notified."

"Moms Goodtime?"

"This was supposed to have been arranged by our local man," explained Sand, grinning. "We've been hearing nothing but good reports on the quality of your merchandise. We'll look your stock over and if it's as good as we expect, we'll place an order for one hundred."

"A hundred?" The lizard pimp swallowed, lowered his rifle. "You want to buy a hundred floozies?"

"Moms Goodtime always buys in quantity," explained Sand. "That's how we keep our prices down and our quality up. With over three hundred Moms Goodtime bordellos in the Hellquad System alone, we naturally have to—"

"Actually we don't have anything like a hundred on hand," said the pimp, uneasy. "See, dude, we just set up our operation in this location. Since we get most of our stock from lightning raids on villages and travelers' parties, it takes awhile to—"

"Perhaps, sir, we ought to move on," said Munson. "These chaps really don't sound as though they can provide us with anything like the—"

"Wait now," said Sand. "I want to give them a chance. After all, these smaller operations may grow and that's why Moms Goodtime likes to encourage the little guy."

"How's about twenty-three?" asked the lizard pimp anxiously.

Sand raised an eyebrow. "Twenty-three? That's all you have on hand?"

"If you could give us a few days, there's a girls school picnic coming up next—"

"Really, sir, I doubt we can do business with such a small potatoes operation."

"Suppose I talk to the boss," said Sand. "Could be we can work out—"

"Sure, right." The lizard man put a green hand rich with jeweled rings on Sand's elbow. "We'll take you in to see Graveyard Slim right now. He's the head man, Mr. . . . ?"

"Sand."

"Mr. Sand. C'mon and talk to Graveyard Slim. He's over in the People's & Robots' Savings Bank, which we're using as our temporary headquarters."

Munson said, "I doubt a chap with the name of Graveyard Slim possesses the business acumen to—"

"Slim's shrewd."

Sand stroked his chin. "What the hell, Munson," he said. "Let's give these fellas a chance."

"We appreciate it," said the lizard pimp.

• • •

Graveyard Slim was a lanky human, clad in a one-piece crimson funsuit. He sat behind a large plazdesk, feet up on it. "There's an interesting yarn, you know, as to how I came to get my nickname," he told them.

"Good gravy," said Munson, who was sitting in a skyblue client chair. "Will we never get down to business?"

Sand grinned across at Slim. "We are in something of a hurry," he said amiably.

"It is an interesting story, though. I mean, you know, I was christened Norbert C. Beethoven." Slim lowered his feet to the carpeted floor. "Something else almost equally interesting is what the C. in the middle there stands for. You could guess a week and never hit the right answer."

Sand came a few steps nearer the desk. The three of them were gathered in the huge ground floor president's office of the abandoned bank. "What Moms Goodtime is more interested in, Slim, is whether you can become a regular supplier for us."

Slim sat up straight. "You mean sell you tarts and hookers every month?"

"Every week."

"Zowie!"

"Exactly," agreed Sand. "First off, though, tell us how many men you have in the brotherhood here at the moment?"

"Well, only just thirteen. But we've got one hell of a waiting list and I could get it up to twenty in a jiffy."

"Really, sir, this is such a pipsqueak operation that it won't ever be able to—"

"How many young ladies do you have on hand at the moment, Slim?"

"Oh, about two dozen. But we can go gather a lot more if—"

"Where do you keep them?"

"We're using the old vault in the basement to store them in." Slim got up. "Come along and I'll show you the whole kaboodle. Each and every one is a real looker. And we just got in a redhead who, although she's a bit feisty right now, is a potential—"

"Before we check out your inventory," said Sand, "my associate and I would like, as rapidly as possible, to meet all your members. Thirteen of them, did you say?"

"Including me, yes." He glanced from Sand to Munson and then back to Sand. "Why do you want to take a gander at—"

"Moms Goodtime is a highly successful operation," Sand said patiently. "We've grown, winning domination of a very competitive field, because we pay attention to details. The quality of the men you have in your organization tells us what we can expect in other areas, Slim."

"Well, you know, some of the guys ain't much to look at," admitted Slim. "For instance, my sister's husband, Leroy, is sort of a—"

"One at a time, sir, would be best I think." Munson rose, producing a packet of file cards and an electric pencil from his pocket.

"Yes, I agree," said Sand. "Slim, would you give the order to have your men come in here one by one, please."

Slim shrugged. "I guess it won't hurt." He leaned down, snapped on his desk intercom. "Jigger, round up the boys and tell them to gather in the lobby and come into my office as they're sent for. Okay? Huh? No, I guess the guards can stay on—"

"We'll want to interview them all," said Sand.

"Make that everybody, Jigger." He turned off the intercom unit. "What exactly will happen when each guy comes in?"

"Show him, Munson."

Munson crossed over and stood next to Slim. After removing his glove, he placed his left little finger under the tip of the slaver's nose.

Hizzzzzzzz!

Bluish mist went climbing into Slim's nostrils.

"You dirty double . . ." His eyes snapped shut, he swayed back and forth once, then fell over atop his desk.

"He will be out cold for at least twelve hours, sir."

"Now we'll never know what his middle name is," said Sand.

Chapter 22

Bare feet, slippered feet and booted feet sounded on the floor of the underground corridor as the captive women hurried out of the open vault and away.

Glory Forbes was the last out of the round-doored room. "Thanks, Sand," she said, pausing on the threshold.

"Wanted to talk with you." He walked beside her up the slanting corridor floor.

"I've been offering to talk with you ever since we first bumped into each other," the red-haired reporter said. "Instead you've had me doped, sabotaged—"

"That was only after you fritzed my andy."

"The heck it was. You started the whole shabby business of playing dirty tricks on—"

"Okay," he said as they crossed the lobby of the bank. "The thing is, Glory, I've figured out what's going on."

"That sure puts you one jump ahead of me." The glaz door slid open in anticipation of her exit.

Outside the freed young women were scattering, disappearing into the gray smoky midday. Munson, arms folded, stood beside the landjeep and watched.

"Let's walk to the park," suggested Sand.

"There's a park?"

"Just around the corner, spotted it coming in."

The park was a half block square, a mixture of neatly planted trees and unattended grass. Bright weeds were thick everywhere, vines festooned the white benches.

When they were seated on the bench nearest the entrance, Glory asked him, "How'd you overcome all those guys?"

He tapped the side of his head. "Ingenuity," he replied. "Along with sleepgas."

"Well, even though I don't much like you, Sand, I appreciate your springing me."

Sand said, "I read your story in the *Galactic Enquirer*."

"I'm flattered," she said. "Hope I didn't upset you too much by getting to Julia Brandywine ahead of you."

"We had three possibilities." He stretched his legs out, bootheels digging into the mossy ground. "Three young women who might be Julia. Turns out she was the one who came here to Fumaza after escaping from Moms Goodtime."

"She's had a rough life since, which is why—"

"I have a packet," he said, tapping his breast pocket, "that contains all her prints."

"She's the real Brandywine daughter. I can vouch—"

"Why do you want them all to converge here on Fumaza, Julia?"

"I don't want . . . why'd you call me that, Sand?"

"Back at the bank they have an ID machine, to clear folks who wanted to cash offplanet checks," he said. "We can use that to match these prints against yours. You've had your face altered quite a bit, dyed your hair. But there's no way you can alter your retinal patterns or your brainscan patterns."

Glory rested her palms on her knees. "Okay, I'm Julia Brandywine," she said. "Now what?"

"Depends," he said. "Why'd you lead us all here?"

"I had a few more things to find out about myself," she told him. "I tagged along with you originally, after persuading my bosses to let me cover the Brandywine story, because you're the least crooked and nasty of the agents involved in the hunt for me. I wanted to know exactly who was coming after me and why. Then I worked things to make certain you'd all converge on the villa near Mount Branco. Getting grabbed by Graveyard Slim and his goons threw me off some, but I think I can still get back there in time to—"

"Your parents are on Fumaza by now. Did you know that?"

"No, but I was expecting they might be." She sighed quietly. "I was hoping they wouldn't come, but of course they'd have to."

"They could've relied on me to locate you."

"You're only window dressing, Sand, to make them look legit," she said. "But they'd never let you get to the secret ahead of me."

"You really have the Death 7 secret?"

"Wait until I make my speech at the villa," Glory said. "Up until recently I wasn't even certain it was my mother and father who'd had that planted in my skull. I'd done a lot of digging into their life and . . .

Oh, I see. You noticed that Julia in my article talked about them just the way I did."

"Yep, that was one thing," he said.

"If they'd stayed dead, I guess I wouldn't have . . . Well, no, I'm not certain," she said. "Probably I'd have begun agitating to have them revived. I really want to talk to them, to find out why they did this to me."

"Most times," said Sand, "you never find out much in situations like this. Even if you do confront them, you—"

"I have to do it," she said. "From the moment my real memory started coming back, I've wanted to know about them. How could they have done what they did, knowing what would happen to me if they were caught? How could they have—"

"They didn't much care about you," said Sand. "So why not forget about facing them and—"

"And what? Who'll you deliver me to? The Political Espionage Office, the central Barnum government, the—"

"Nobody. SOF already paid me for this job," he said. "You go on being Glory Forbes, I get back to my vacation."

"What'll that do? Micro isn't going to give up until he hunts me down, Typhoon Tyson won't either and neither will my loving parents, Sand. Nothing's over until—"

"You're a good reporter. Stick with that and forget—"

"I'm not going to quit that. I am Glory Forbes now and I'll stay Glory Forbes," she said. "Yes, I know it's a flashy name. I picked it for myself when I was still young and . . . well, not innocent after Moms Goodtime . . . but naive. I like the name, though."

Sand said, "You remember your parents."

"Yes, it was only ten years ago that they were executed."

"Did you like them much then?"

Glory looked away from him. "Not much, no. I was already wound up in my own ambitions, trying to write and break free of—"

"Then you can pretty much figure what they'll say when and if you do face them."

"Even so, Sand, I am going to do it. I . . . I'd like you to help me."

"Going to be risky, with Micro and Tyson in on this, too."

"I want to have them all in one place when—"

"But youse don't, kid." Strangler Selznick stepped from behind a tree. In his right hand he held Micro's silvery jug, in his left a kilgun. "That bug in your fanny got us pretty damn close before it went flooey, Sand."

"Focus," repeated Micro. "Do something right for a change, thumbs."

"Geeze, boss, youse oughtn't to chew me out in front of company." Strangler made another small adjustment to the lens attached to the side of the jug. "Dere, dat's nice and sharp."

"I still look as though I'm coated with fuzz."

"It's da smoke in da air, no kidding."

They'd herded Sand and Glory into an office building near the park. Micro's jug was perched atop a desk and an enlarged image of him was being projected on the nearest wall.

"There's a squiggly line down my middle."

"Dat's just a crack in da plazter, boss."

Micro, now fully three feet high on the wall, was a thin nervous man of thirty-five. Sharp-featured, with straight brown hair and black-rimmed sunglasses. He wore a two-piece white bizsuit.

Sand nodded at the jug. "What'd you gents do with my android?"

"Ain't youse worried about dat jungle bimbo and the gink with the frizzy hair, too?"

"Wasn't sure you knew about them."

"Geeze, I ain't dat dumb, Sand. I spotted dem right off in da jungle trying to ambush us. Took care of 'em just like dat." He snapped his beefy fingers.

Sand moved closer to him. "Took care of them how?"

"Don't get your bowels in a snood. Da boss said I was only just to stun 'em."

"Might we get on with our business," said Micro from his jug. His projected image showed him pacing impatiently. "Miss Forbes, or rather Miss Brandywine, you've eluded me long enough. I want the secret of Death 7."

"What makes you think she's Julia Brandywine?" asked Sand.

"We overheard youse talking about it. So knock off the bluff crapola, huh?"

Glory brushed her red hair back from her face. "Who're you working for, Micro?"

"That's really none of your—"

"My parents?"

His amplified laugh was thin and nasal. "I don't work for amateurs," he told her. "My client is . . . a planet alliance that I won't mention. All this is wasting time. Strangler, get the surgical kit."

Sand coughed. There was considerable volcanic smoke getting into the room despite the still functioning aircirc system. "What the hell are you planning to do?"

"The information I want is planted in her head,"

answered Micro. "Simplest way to get it is to open her skull and remove it."

"Here and now?"

"I'm certainly not going to transport her all the way to my clients' home planets for the job."

"You'll kill her if you—"

"Youse got to cure yerself of dis maudlin streak, Sand. You'd be a pretty fair agent if youse didn't act like a sob sister every . . . Holy H. Crow!"

The floor began to wobble, the walls were shaking.

"Mount Branco," said Glory close beside Sand.

The tremors grew worse. The walls groaned, the office furniture started hopping and jumping.

"Catch me!" cried Micro as his jug bounced across the desk and dropped off.

His image was projected on the ceiling, the wall, the floor.

Sand pushed Glory back. "Stay clear."

He sprinted, reached the jug just as it hit the rug. He brought his foot up, booted the jug hard.

Micro's amplified scream came snapping out of the jug.

The jug flew up smack into Strangler's face, hitting him along the nose and across the mouth.

"Youse is a viper!" he growled, stumbling back.

Micro's jug hit the floor again, bounced twice, once again, and went rolling across the undulating floor and into a wall.

Cracks were snaking up the walls, the ceiling beams were shaking.

"Get outside," Sand yelled to the girl.

He moved in on Strangler, who was offbalance and slumped.

Sand dodged in, dealt him a chopping blow to the side of the neck. Hit him twice more.

"Youse crummy . . . oof!"

Sand punched him in the midsection.

Strangler folded, swinging out wildly as he dropped to his knees.

The ceiling made a crumbling sound and large chunks of it began raining down. A heavy hunk of plazter and neowood slammed Sand across the back. He stumbled, fell against the desk.

The floor was shaking and the desk started rolling him against a wall.

Sand edged clear of it, spun and went running for the door.

Nearly there he tripped over a fallen ceiling beam.

He fell flat out several yards from the way out.

"Here, c'mon." Glory came back into the collapsing room, took hold of Sand's arm and yanked him along with her.

They were in the middle of the street when the entire ceiling of the room they'd been in collapsed.

"Keep moving," said Sand.

They ran toward the park area, brix and jagged fragments of building surface falling and bouncing all around them.

The trees in the park were jerking from side to side, branches crackling. All at once the earth opened and a wide crevice formed and zigzagged across the center of the weedy parkgrounds.

Sand caught Glory around the waist, kept her from running on into the deepening opening.

Thick smoke was rolling through the rattling streets, yellow and filled with sparks and swirls of soot.

Things kept falling down.

Sand had stopped running, stood holding the red-haired girl.

"Think we'll make it?" she said.

He shrugged. "We're doing better than Micro and Strangler."

Gradually the ground stopped shaking, the debris ceased to come tumbling down.

Smoky silence closed in.

Chapter
23

"Double rosco!" Barni Sutt came bounding out of her cottage, braided blue hair flicking. "I knew it was true love between you two and now you've gone and rescued Glory from the clutches of gosh knows what and brought her back in triumph. Zappo!"

Sand had parked the landjeep on the yellow gravel drive next to the brix cottage. "I have two people in back here who have to be put in your infirmary," he said, walking toward her. "Both stungunned. Also got an android who's had a mild disabler shock and needs a minor tuneup. I can handle that if—"

"Boy, you two must've had some terrific adventures out there in the teeming wilderness. You come back with your battlescarred vehicle piled high with maimed and wounded, the—"

"Barni," said Glory as she crossed over to her from the jeep, "the infirmary here is still functioning, isn't it?"

"Heck yes Our structures are built to withstand shocks, tremors, eruptions and all. Except for Uncle Mel's indoor swimming pool, which isn't anymore, we came through the whole thing okay."

Glory pointed at a large blue-domed building across the clearing. "John, you can take Sargasso and Lorna over there to—"

"Zappo! Is that Lorna the Jungle Girl?" Barni scurried over to the jeep, peering into the back seat at the two people slumped there. "Are you sure?"

Sand eased back behind the wheel. "Where's the workshop?"

"Double barf," remarked Barni. "She's awfully old looking. I thought a jungle girl would be young, lovely to look at and petite. That's a zunky fur she's wearing too."

"There's a repair shop in that green building," said Glory. "You can patch up Munson there, John."

"One requires . . . little in the way of repairs," muttered the android, who was stretched out on the floor of the vehicle. "One is more hurt by . . . the indignity . . . of traveling about like . . . a bundle of wetwash . . ."

"I'll see," said Sand, restarting the engine, "that everyone is looked after."

"I won't do anything until you come back," promised Glory. "Really."

Grinning, Sand drove off.

"Zappo!" observed Barni. "This is really terribly romantic."

The villa sat in a clearing surrounded by thick green jungle. Several bedraggled blue parrots were perched on the high branches of the nearest trees, chattering, bickering, comparing notes. You could see Moun

Branco in the distance, sending yellowish smoke up into the late afternoon.

Glory and Sand were on a slight rise from which they could watch the sewdostucco house down through the trees.

"Seems as though that's all we're going to get," the redhead said.

Nodding, Sand rose up off the mossy ground. "Yep, everybody who's still alive and hunting for you has arrived." He brushed a fuzzy green bug from his trouser leg.

Glory took a deep breath. "Okay, we may as well go on in."

"Now seems like about the right time." Stungun in hand, he escorted her down toward the villa where Julia Brandywine was supposed to be hiding.

"They're the same as they were then, no older," Glory said as they descended through the brush. "My father and mother, but they looked a lot different."

"They've been suspended. You haven't." His elbow brushed a stand of pink bamboo, starting it to rattle.

From out in the courtyard you could already hear them inside.

". . . damn well the PEO has jurisdiction," Typhoon Tyson was insisting. "If this damn daughter of yours turns up here, we get the secret and not you."

"We didn't come back to life . . . and let me tell you that was a very painful experience . . . and travel all these weary miles to this godforsaken planet," said the voice of Hazel Brandywine, "to have our only child snatched away from us."

"Hogwash," countered the big Political Espionage Office agent. "You two are spies, traitors to your native planet system."

"On the contrary, Mr. Tyson," Jonas Brandywine

pointed out. "We're decent citizens, wrongly accused, framed by sinister forces. It clearly states that right here in the papers they handed us when we awoke."

"I know what those damn papers say. I helped draft them," said Tyson loudly. "That's a lot of garbage, as we all know. You are guilty, you did swipe Gobblinn's secret."

"That makes no difference," persisted Jonas. "According to our attorney, we've been cleared for good and all. No matter what you PEO people think, no matter what the truth is, we can not be executed again, Mr. Tyson. That would be double jeopardy."

"Listen, if you two try to keep me from getting the secret of Death 7, I'll see that you end up either dead or the next best thing."

Hazel saw her first, standing framed in the doorway to the large living room. "Baby," she said in a faint voice. "It's my baby Julia, isn't it?"

Jonas was staring at Glory. "Yes, Hazel, I believe it is. Yes."

Hazel walked across the neowood floor, put her arms, carefully, around Glory. "I don't like your new face as well as the old one, but I know it's you. A mother you can never fool," she said, kissing her on each cheek in turn. "I suppose you like this new face, dear, and the color of your hair? Myself I'd have picked a quieter shade, but it's your hair after all." Hugging her once more, she stepped clear. "You're twenty-one now, so it's—"

"Twenty-three," said Glory quietly.

Hazel lowered her head, began to cry softly. "Ten years apart."

Jonas moved now. He crossed the room, put his arm around his wife's shoulders. "No need to cry, mother," he said. "We're all together again. Aren't we, Julia."

Glory moved around them and into the room. "Hello, Tyson."

The PEO agent grunted. "I see you brought that bastard Sand along with you. Sand, your butt's in a real sling over what you did to me aboard the *Space Queen*," he said. "Soon as I clear this mess up I'm—"

"No, you're not," Sand told him as he came into the room. "You don't want to answer to all the charges I could bring. And with SOF's dough behind me, I can drag you folks into half the courts in the Barnum System."

"What charges? Buddy, you interfered with an agent of the—"

"Hold it," suggested Glory. "Let's all sit down and talk."

"Is this young man a friend of yours?" Hazel inclined her head at Sand. "He looks a little roughedged and nasty, but I suppose I've no right anymore to pass judgment on your beaus."

"He's not my beau." Glory sat on one side of the low plaz sofa. "He's John Wesley Sand."

"Oh, the man who's working for us." Jonas studied him up and down. "Well, when you do business at a distance you can't expect—"

"Don't be too critical, dear," cautioned his wife. "Most freelance agents have to be mean and—"

"Sit down," repeated Glory. "Please."

Grinning thinly, Sand seated himself next to her. "Yes, ma'am."

"What the blue blazes do you think you're going to pull off here, Sand?" Tyson, reluctantly, lowered himself to the edge of a slingchair. "Have an auction maybe? Well, let me point out, buddy, that Dr. Hugo Gobblinn was employed by the government of Barnum when he perfected Death 7. Therefore, anything he developed or invented is automatically the property of—"

"She's our daughter," reminded Jonas, guiding his wife to the other sofa. "Before you touch her, Mr. Tyson, you must have our permission. And that, I can assure you, is going to cost you."

Glory took hold of Sand's hand, squeezed it, let go. "You really don't control me, father."

"Hell, I'll negotiate directly with you," Tyson told her. "Even though you're carrying a stolen government secret around in your skull, we'd be willing to pay you something for it. Not an enormous sum obviously, since what with recent budget cuts all down the—"

"Julia, you're a grownup lady now," said Hazel. "I can see that. But still, dear, you're our child and if there's money paid for this secret, we ought to share in—"

"I got my memory back several years ago," said Glory, not looking at any of them. "The government brainwipe wasn't very effective, which, I later found out, is true of a good many of—"

"We've got the best damn identity changing setup in the uni—"

"Let her speak her piece, Tyson," said Jonas. "Then we can get down to haggling over price."

Tyson made a grumbling sound.

"I remembered who I really was," continued Glory. "And what had been done to me. Eventually, since my memory came back gradually, I even recalled your taking me to a bootleg surgeon, father, and having something planted inside my head. I . . . that memory was a long time in coming back. You never did tell me the truth about the operation, but once I started digging into your case I realized what it must've been."

"You were a child then," said her mother "you wouldn't really have wanted to know the truth."

"We fully expected," explained her father, "to get away with all this, dear. In time we'd have removed the dot of information, sold it and everything would've worked out just fine."

Glory said, looking at her parents now, "I could've contacted you on Esmeralda the moment you were revived. But instead—"

"I've been wondering about that," said Hazel. "After all, not that we're complaining, but since your memory, as you now tell us, had returned some time—"

"The reason I didn't," she said, "was that I wanted you to come out here to the Hellquad. I wanted you to see the planets I'd grown up on."

"You had it rough," acknowledged her father. "But then so did we, Julia."

"I wanted to have you here," Glory went on, "you and everyone who was interested in the Gobblinn formula so—"

"But everyone isn't here. Micro's on your tail, too, and he's not—"

"Defunct," said Sand.

"Huh?"

"Micro's dead and gone. He and Strangler both," Sand said. "Tragic accident."

"Why the hell didn't you menti—"

"Let her go on," said Jonas.

"When I decided to have my appearance changed," said Glory, "I contacted a doctor on . . . that doesn't matter. He was a good man, especially considering his outlaw status. Before he went to work he took X rays and did brainscans. He noticed that microdot of information you'd had planted in my head for safe keeping, father. For no extra charge, after he asked me what I wanted done, he removed it."

"Where the devil is it?" Tyson hopped to his feet.

"Let her explain," said Hazel.

Glory said, "I destroyed it. Years ago."

"Death 7? You destroyed the secret of Death 7, one of the most powerful and deadly weapons ever conceived?" Tyson's hands kept flexing into fists.

"Are you teasing us, Julia?" asked her mother. "You liked to play jokes when you were—"

"Not a joke, not a prank." She stood up. "The secret of Death 7 hasn't existed for years."

"Julia, you put us through all this expense and bother," said her father sadly, "just to—"

"Just so I could say good-bye." Glory walked out of the room and into the hazy late afternoon.

Only Sand followed her.

DAW

Presenting JOHN NORMAN in DAW editions . . .

] **HUNTERS OF GOR** (#UE1678–$2.75)
] **MARAUDERS OF GOR** (#UE1901–$2.95)
] **TRIBESMEN OF GOR** (#UE1893–$3.50)
] **SLAVE GIRL OF GOR** (#UE1904–$3.50)
] **BEASTS OF GOR** (#UE1903–$3.50)
] **EXPLORERS OF GOR** (#UE1905–$3.50)
] **FIGHTING SLAVE OF GOR** (#UE1882–$3.50)
] **ROGUE OF GOR** (#UE1892–$3.50)
] **GUARDSMAN OF GOR** (#UE1890–$3.50)
] **SAVAGES OF GOR** (#UE1715–$3.50)
] **BLOOD BROTHERS OF GOR** (#UE1777–$3.50)
] **KAJIRA OF GOR** (#UE1807–$3.50)
] **PLAYERS OF GOR** (#UE1914–$3.50)
] **TIME SLAVE** (#UE1761–$2.50)
] **IMAGINATIVE SEX** (#UE1912–$2.95)
] **GHOST DANCE** (#UE1633–$2.75)

With over four million copies of DAW's John Norman books in print, these enthralling novels are in constant demand. They combine heroic adventure, interplanetary peril, and the in-depth depiction of Earth's counter-orbital twin with a special charm all their own.

AW BOOKS are represented by the publishers of Signet nd Mentor Books, NEW AMERICAN LIBRARY

EW AMERICAN LIBRARY
0. Box 999, Bergenfield, New Jersey 07621

ease send me the DAW BOOKS I have checked above. I am enclosing
_____ (check or money order—no currency or C.O.D.'s).
lease include the list price plus $1.00 per order to cover handling
osts.

ame _____

ddress _____

ity _____ State _____ Zip Code _____
Please allow at least 4 weeks for delivery

DAW
SCIENCE
FICTION

A GALAXY OF SCIENCE FICTION STARS!

LEE CORREY Manna	UE1896—$2.95
TIMOTHY ZAHN The Blackcollar	UE1843—$2.95
A.E. VAN VOGT Computerworld	UE1879—$2.50
COLIN KAPP Search for the Sun	UE1858—$2.25
ROBERT TREBOR An XT Called Stanley	UE1865—$2.50
ANDRE NORTON Horn Crown	UE1635—$2.95
JACK VANCE The Face	UE1921—$2.50
E.C. TUBB Angado	UE1908—$2.50
KENNETH BULMER The Diamond Contessa	UE1853—$2.50
ROGER ZELAZNY Deus Irae	UE1887—$2.50
PHILIP K. DICK Ubik	UE1859—$2.50
DAVID J. LAKE Warlords of Xuma	UE1832—$2.50
CLIFFORD D. SIMAK Our Children's Children	UE1880—$2.50
M.A. FOSTER Transformer	UE1814—$2.50
GORDON R. DICKSON Mutants	UE1809—$2.95
BRIAN STABLEFORD The Gates of Eden	UE1801—$2.50
JOHN BRUNNER The Jagged Orbit	UE1917—$2.95
EDWARD LLEWELLYN Salvage and Destroy	UE1898—$2.95
PHILIP WYLIE The End of the Dream	UE1900—$2.25

NEW AMERICAN LIBRARY
P.O. Box 999, Bergenfield, New Jersey 07621

Please send me the DAW BOOKS I have checked above. I am enclosing
$_____ (check or money order—no currency or C.O.D.'s).
Please include the list price plus $1.00 per order to cover handling
costs.

Name _____

Address _____

City _____ State _____ Zip Code _____

Please allow at least 4 weeks for delivery